This book is dedicated to my uncle, Gregory McCarthy, may you rest in peace. You always looked after me as a kid, even when I did wrong. I love and respect you for that. You will always be missed and will forever be my favorite uncle. I know you're looking after me. Love you, Unc.

Unique
Written By: Richard Warren

Written by: Richard Warren
Phone #: 860.913.0990
Email: hoodlit@gmail.com
Website: www.hoodlit.com
Facebook: Richard McCarthy

Formatted by: O'Connor Legal, Medical & Media Services LLC
Phone #: 860.266.2601
Email: sales@oconnorlmms.com
Website: www.oconnorlmms.com
***This book was formatted as per the author's instructions.
Urban jargon was not edited in order to keep the context of the
book consistent.***

Chapter 1

Melony and Candy hung out at Unique's condo out in South Windsor, smoking purple haze. Candy's cell phone hadn't stopped ringing since they got there.

"Damn, Candy, who blowing ya shit up like that?" Melony asked.

Candy looked at her cell phone and sucked her teeth.

"That ain't nobody but Rondell's stalking ass. Some niggas just don't know when it's over," Candy replied.

"Candy must got that good-good. He can't get enough of you."

"You know it. But I'm done with his ass," Candy replied, as she cut her phone off.

The ladies' conversation was cut short when D-Red walked into the house with his boy, Calvin. Unique greeted her man, as soon as he walked through the door.

"Hey, baby," Unique said.

"What's up, love?" D-Red replied, before walking into their bedroom and opening up his safe.

He took money out of the duffel bag and stacked it neatly into his safe. Unique walked into their bedroom.

"Baby, I need some money," Unique said.

"When don't you need some money?" D-Red asked.

"Me and my girls' going to Divi Divis."

"You gone get enough of that death trap."

"Boy, Divi Divis is not no death trap," Unique stated.

"Let you tell it."

D-Red passed her a stack of cash.

"Thanks, baby," Unique said, before kissing him on the lips.

D-Red admired her big round ass bounce from side-to-side, as she walked out of the room. He wouldn't trade her sexy chocolate ass in for nothing in the world. Unique had been with him since back in the days. D-Red knew her since she was a dirty little girl in the hood begging for dollars.

He wasn't too crisp his self, until he started selling dope. D-Red didn't waste his time selling any other type of drug. He knew that there was no other money like dope money. Unique and her girls got in Unique's Benz CLK that D-Red had bought her for her birthday.

"We going out tonight," Unique said.

"I don't got it right now to be going out," Melony replied.

"Girl, I got y'all. Let's go see Mega," Unique said.

When they walked into the Wreck Shop, all eyes were on them. Candy was a petite redbone with thick thighs and hips, a fat ass, pretty face, long Indian hair like Pocahontas, and a handful of breasts. Unique was a sexy chocolate chick with long baby hair, cat eyes, slim waist, perky breasts, a nice and round onion, and a face that resembled Rudy from *The Cosby Show*.

Every time she stepped in a room, all eyes were on her. Melony was a slim, sexy, brown-skinned chick. She had breasts the size of melons, and a body like a runway model.

"Hi, Mega," the ladies said, as they walked into the Wreck Shop.

2

"What's up, ladies? What can I do for y'all today?" Mega asked.

"We trying to get some tickets to see Jadakiss," Unique said.

"It's $180 for three tickets."

Unique paid for their tickets before looking around for an outfit to wear. She saw a Moschino outfit that looked perfect on her. Melony saw a Baby Phat outfit that she liked. And Candy decided to copp an Apple Bottom outfit that hugged her body just right. When they left the Wreck Shop, they jumped back in the whip.

"We need some weed before we go to the show," Unique said.

"Go through Uptown so I can see Will's tricking ass. You know he like me and be giving me free weed," Melony said.

"Shit, the way he be sweating you, Melony, I would be getting more than some free weed from his ass," Unique replied.

"I know that's right," Candy added.

When they pulled up on Uptown, Will was sitting in a cherry red Honda coupe with chrome rims. Unique pulled on the side of Will's car. He rolled down the window and smoke came out the window.

"What up, Will?" Melony asked.

"Ain't shit; out here doing my numbers," Will replied.

"You got bud?" Melony asked.

"Yeah, hop out."

Melony jumped out of the car and walked over to Will's car. The hustlers on the block watched her, with lust in their eyes. Will hung his jeweled-up hand and wrist out his whip and grabbed her by the waist.

"Melony, what's good?" Will asked.

"I need some piff; we about to go see Jadakiss."

"Word?"

"Yeah, he at the Hippodrome tonight," Melony explained.

Will passed her a few bags of bud.

"I might see y'all up there. That's on the house right there."

Melony pushed the weed into her pocket. Her jeans were so tight it was a struggle for her to get the weed inside. Will licked his lips, as he admired her sexy body. Melony smiled, when she saw him watching her.

"What?" Melony asked.

"Girl, you sexy as hell. When you gone stop playing and let me take care of you?"

"Call me," Melony said, before walking away.

When she got back in the whip, they drove to Keney Park, rolled a couple of blunts, and got twisted, while listening to Keyshia Cole. After they smoked a couple piece of haze and drunk a few bottles of Remy Martin, Unique dropped them off. As soon as Candy walked through her door, her phone was ringing.

"Hello," Candy said.

"Bitch, where the hell you been at all day?" Rondell yelled into the phone.

"See? Huh-uh! Who the hell you calling a bitch?

"I'm talking to ya high yellow ass! Now, come open the door! I'm in the front!"

Candy hung up the phone in Rondell's ear and sucked her teeth. She was tired of him disrespecting her and wasn't gone put up with it no more. As she sat on the arm of her couch in heavy thought, she heard Rondell beating down the door. Candy jumped.

"Bitch, open the fucking door!" Rondell yelled, from the other side of the door.

"I'm calling the cops! You better get the hell out of here!" Candy yelled.

All of a sudden, the beating stopped. Candy sighed because she really feared for her life and didn't know what Rondell would do next.

*   *   *

Melony walked into her mother's apartment in West Brook with her daughter, Kiara, by her side.

"Mama, can you watch Kiara while I go out?" Melony asked.

"Melony, when you gone stop club hopping and settle down with a good man?" Ms. Watkins asked.

"Mama, I'm happy being single. I don't need a man."

"Child, every woman needs a good man in their life. Trust me. I know."

"Mama, I'll see you later. Thanks for watching Kiara," Melony replied.

"Uh-huh," her mother replied, as Melony walked out the door.

Melony tried to brush off what her mother had just said, but the statement she made about every woman needing a good man kept running through her head.

*   *   *

When they picked up Candy, she jumped in the car with a frustrated look on her face.

"What's wrong?" Unique asked.

"After you dropped me off, me and Rondell got into an argument on the phone. And the next thing I know, his crazy ass is beating my door down, talking about let him in," Candy said.

"See? Huh-uh, you need to call the cops on his ass. That nigga is 7:30 for real," Unique replied.

"You know how I feel about the Police."

"Well, you need to get you a gun," Melony added.

"Girl, ain't no gun store selling me no gun, not with my record."

"Shit, you don't need no gun store to get a strap. I can pull up on any one of these corners and get you a banger," Melony replied.

"I don't know.

"Don't think too long. It might cost you your life."

Candy turned the music back up, not wanting to talk about guns and Rondell anymore. Club Hippodrome was packed with ballers, hustlers, pimps, players, and fly girls. Everybody who was somebody was in the building. As the ladies stepped through the club, all eyes were on them. As soon as they walked over to the bar, a young kid no older than 18 walked over to the ladies.

"Hi, I'm JC and I'm here to give you ladies these VIP passes, courtesy of Mr. Ray Black," JC said.

"Thank you, baby," Melony said, as she touched his face.

JC blushed and walked away before the women could see the erection growing in his jeans.

"Who is Mr. Ray Black?" Melony asked.

"The CEO of CT Records; girl, he is paid," Candy said, excitedly.

"Wasn't he in the *XXL*?" Melony asked.

He be in all those hip-hop magazines; him and his team doing big things."

When the ladies walked into VIP, they were guided to a table that was filled with bottles of Ciroc, Ace of Spade, and an assortment of fruit. Melony popped a few grapes in her mouth. Mr. Ray Black walked over.

He was a dark-skinned man with deep waves, pretty boy features, and a muscular build. He worked out on a daily to keep his body toned up. Ladies found him attractive. And on top of that, he was caked up.

"Hello, ladies. My name's Ray Black and I'm the host of this party," Mr. Ray Black said.

"We know who you are," Candy said, with a smile on her face.

Mr. Ray Black showed his pearly whites.

"Well, you ladies enjoy yourselves. And if you need anything, don't hesitate to give me a call," Mr. Ray Black said, as he looked into Melony's eyes and passed her his card.

When Mr. Ray Black left the table, Candy spoke her mind.

"Ooh, girl, he like you, Melony," Candy said.

"He was just being nice," Melony replied.

"Girl, you need to quit," Candy said.

"He was kinda sweating me hard," Melony replied, with a smile on her face.

"So, are you going to call him?"

"I don't know."

"You better. That nigga is paid," Candy said.

"I know that's right," Unique added.

Crook Type hit the stage, interrupting the ladies' conversation. They got up out of their seats and began to dance, as Ville Will spit his gutta lyrics. After Crook Type did their thing and rocked the crowd, Jadakiss, the man everyone had came out to see, came out and put on a hell of a show.

After a few joints off his latest album, the entire D-Block crew came out and spit a few throwback songs. After the club, Candy bumped into Jerome, a kid she had went to school with.

"Candy, what's up, girl? Damn, you looking good," Jerome said.

"Thank you," Candy said, with a smile on her face.

"So, how you been?"

"I been all right. How's Lisa doing?

"We ain't together," Jerome replied.

"That's too bad."

"Enough about Lisa; what's up with me and you? What you trying to get into?"

Candy walked up to Jerome and grabbed his dick, before whispering in his ear, "You think you ready for me?"

Jerome was shocked that Candy was ready to get it popping. Usually when he tried to holla at her, they played the cat-and-mouse game; but not today. Candy was tipsy and needed some good dick in her life. Candy turned to her girls with a smile on her face.

"I'll see y'all tomorrow," Candy said.

"Alright, girl," Melony and Unique said, in unison.

Any other time, Candy would have turned Jerome down because she knew Lisa was a thumper, and she didn't want any drama with the girl. But today was a different story. Lisa was doing 18 months for check fraud and wasn't coming home anytime soon.

Unique and Melony walked into a pizza shop down the block from the club. Hustlers tried to holla as soon as they walked into the pizza shop. The ladies ignored the hustlers and ordered their food. When they got back in the car, Unique spoke her mind.

"Candy finally got up with Jerome," Unique said.

"She always liked him, since high school," Melony replied.

"They make a cute couple."

Melony agreed. Unique put in her *Best of Queens Bridge* CD before she sparked a blunt of piff and drove back to the hood. When Melony got back to her mother's house, she was banging on the door. Ms. Watkins came to the door. Melony ran past her and rushed into the bathroom.

"Girl, what's wrong with you?" Ms. Watkins asked.

"I gotta pee," Melony said.

After Melony used the bathroom, she washed her hands and walked to the room where her daughter, Kiara, was sleeping.

"Kiara," Melony said.

"Yes, mommy," Kiara replied, in a sleepy voice.

"Wake up; we about to go home."

"Leave that child alone. You know I ain't letting her go nowhere this time of night."

"I'll come get her in the morning," Melony stated.

9

"Uh-huh."

Her mother closed the door where Kiara was sleeping.

"Melony, when you gone stop running the streets and settle down with a good man?" Ms. Watkins asked.

"Mama, I don't need no man. And I only go out on the weekends. I work a full-time job and take care of my daughter so she don't need no father."

"That girl need her father in her life."

"A father like daddy; all he ever did was run the streets, cheat, and didn't take care of home," Melony asked.

"You see, that's where you wrong. Your father might have ran the streets. But he made sure to take care of home before any of them tramps got a dime of his money."

"I clearly remember you leaving me with nana when you and him was out playing Bonnie and Clyde."

"Anything we ever did was so you could have a better life," Ms. Watkins said, as tears ran down her face.

"I'm sorry, mama."

Melony hugged her mother, before walking out the door.

*   *   *

Unique walked into her condo a little tipsy. She tripped over a boot, as she stepped into the dark living room.

"I'm gone kick his ass for leaving them damn boots in my living room," Unique said out loud, as she flicked on the light.

10

D-Red was sitting on the couch in the dark.

"Boy, what the hell wrong with you sitting in the dark?" Unique asked.

"How was Divi Divis?" D-Red asked.

"We ain't go. We went to the Hippodrome to see Jadakiss."

"I know."

"You was there?" Unique questioned.

"Nope, I got eyes all over, though."

"You tell them hating-ass bitches I know I'm beautiful. But, damn, stop watching me."

"Bring ya sexy ass here, girl," D-Red said, as he grabbed her by the waist and pulled her up onto his lap. They started kissing. It wasn't long before they were making love.

*   *   *

Candy and Jerome were all over each other, as soon as they were inside of Jerome's penthouse. Candy fell back on the bed, as Jerome hopped on top of her and kissed her body. He had her out of her clothes in seconds. Jerome spread her thick thighs and began to lick on her clit.

"Right there! Yes!" Candy moaned, as she grabbed the back of his head.

Jerome ate her out until she couldn't hold back any longer and began squirting like a waterfall. Jerome was rock hard, as he tasted her juices. He grabbed her by the waist and penetrated her box. As he dug all up in her guts, she scratched up his back. Jerome was giving her

11

what she yearned for. And Candy was loving every minute of it.

"Oh, yes! Fuck me!" Candy moaned, as he beat the pussy up.

Jerome stroked her fast, and then slow, giving her the best of both worlds. Candy began to climax for the second time. Jerome came right along with her. His body began to convulse, as he skeeted on her six-pack abs.

Candy and Jerome took a shower together. She washed his body down, getting him aroused again. She dropped down to her knees and sucked him off, until he skeeted on her tonsils. When she swallowed his babies, that blew his mind.

Chapter 2

Monito stood in front of the buildings on Belden Street, running sales for D-Red, when a white boy pulled up in a black Monte Carlo SS.

"You got boy?" The white boy asked.

Monito looked at the white boy suspiciously.

"I never seen you around here before," Monito said.

"I copp from Woody all the time; I need six bundles. But I want to see the big man."

"I don't know nobody named Woody," Monito replied, before walking in the hallway where D-Red was at. "Boss, I got a white boy outside who wants six bundles. But he only wants to deal with who's in charge," Monito said.

"Tell him ain't nothing popping. He's the Feds."

"You sure; he's spending big money, pai."

"Do it, Monito."

Monito walked over to where the white boy was parked, counting money.

"Ain't nothing jumping!" Monito said.

"Come on, man. I'm spending good money."

"Keep it moving, Policia."

The Narc pulled off when he realized his cover had been blown. A few minutes later, a burgundy Buick Regal with dirty darks pulled up on the block. The passenger's side window rolled down.

"Hey, man! Tell D-Red that Silk and Ghetto out here," Ghetto said.

Monito walked back in the hallway where his boss was sitting on the steps, counting cash.

"D-Red, some fools in a red Buick Regal named Silk and Ghetto told me to tell you they outside," Monito said.

D-Red sucked his teeth.

"Tell them niggas to come in the hallway," D-Red replied.

"They giving you static, boss? Because all you gotta do is give me the word and I'll take care of it," Monito said.

"Nah, everything is cool."

Monito went outside and told Silk and Ghetto to come in the hallway. Silk and Ghetto walked in the hallway, looking grimy, dressed in black hoodies, Timbs, skully hats, and Army fatigue coats. Ghetto walked up to D-Red and gave him dap, while Silk leaned against the wall with his hand clutching a fully loaded .50 cal that was in his coat pocket. He had a shiesty look on his face, as the men talked business.

"What's up, playboy?" Ghetto asked.

"Ain't shit, trying to get this money," D-Red replied, before passing Ghetto a wad of cash.

"Same time next week," Ghetto said, before walking out of the building with $3,500 of D-Red's hard-earned cash. Since the fall of the Commission, Silk and Ghetto have been extorting big-wheel hustlers all through the city to stay above water.

*　　*　　*

Monito had grew up on Belden Street. After fighting in Desert Storm, Monito came back home with a bad dope habit and no place to live. His mother had died while he was gone, and she was his only source of income.

D-Red took Monito under his wing and helped him get an apartment on the block, and gave him his old clothes and Timbs when they got scuffed up a little. Monito was grateful for the love D-Red showed him and worked hard for D-Red.

He was on the block day-in and day-out, running sales for D-Red, making him rich. D-Red was never the beefing type. So when Silk and Ghetto started pressing him for cash, he decided it would be smarter for him to pay them instead of going to war. D-Red knew he couldn't beef and get money.

Chapter 3

Unique and Melony was walking into her apartment, when Allstar, a local rapper, stopped her.

"Melony, what's up? You looking right today," Allstar said.

"Thank you," Melony replied.

"So what's up with me and you?"

"Allstar, you're too young for me," Melony said, with a smile on her face.

"All right, now, don't be beating my door down when I blow up in the rap game."

"I wish you the best," Melony replied, before walking into her apartment with Unique.

"Melony, why you waste your time talking to that little nigga? He know not to try to holla at me, because I will shut his ass down," Unique said.

"Allstar is all right. He's just too young. That's all."

"If a nigga ain't got no money, he don't have a shot with me."

"So, if D-Red was broke, you would leave him?" Melony asked.

"You damn right; D-Red knows what I'm accustomed to."

Melony shook her head. Their conversation was cut short when Candy walked through the door.

"What's up, y'all?" Candy asked.

"What's up?" Melony replied.

"So, how did it go with Jerome? I see he had you put up for the last two days," Unique said.

"Girl, it was incredible. Jerome touched and loved me like no other man has in a while," Candy replied.

"So what about Lisa?"

"He said it's over."

"Does she know that?" Unique questioned.

"He's waiting for the right time to tell her."

"Don't let him have his cake and eat it, too. Make him end it with her," Melony said.

"I will."

Unique dumped the guts of a Garcia Vega out and filled it with Kush. She sparked the blunt and looked at Melony.

"So, Melony, did you call Mr. Ray Black?" Unique asked.

"Nah," Melony replied.

"Why not?"

"That man probably got girls chasing him all over the country. I'm good," Melony replied.

"He might not, though," Candy added.

"I don't need a man right now. As long as I got my Hood Lit Publishing collection of books by Richard Warren, I'm good," Melony replied, as she looked at a picture of the author in the back of *Stick Up Kids is Out to Play*.

"He is fine," Unique added.

"His chocolate ass can definitely get it," Candy replied, as she grabbed the blunt from Unique and looked at his picture.

*   *   *

Rondell screwed up his face, as Candy sent him to voicemail. To say he was heated would be an understatement. Candy had kicked him to the curb, and he wanted her back desperately. A porno flick played on the television screen inside his hotel room. And it wasn't long before he began to pleasure his self, while thinking about Candy.

Chapter 4

Calvin sat parked on Belden Street, observing the fiends go in and out his drug gate. Money had been coming fast, and he had workers on the block around the clock. When D-Red wasn't out there, Calvin held it down for his partner in crime.

D-Red and Calvin had been friends since grade school. And they both started selling dope around the same time. D-Red was a lot more flashy with his cash than Calvin. Calvin was more low key. He knew the dope hustle was a vicious game.

And not only did he have to watch the haters, but he had Police, jouk boys, and gold diggers to keep his eye on, as well. Calvin's Nextel begin to ring.

"Hello?" Calvin said.

"Bay, where you at?" Trinicia asked.

"On the block, what's up?"

"You coming through tonight?"

"Yeah, I'll be there in a minute," Calvin replied.

"Call me when you outside."

"All right, I got you," Calvin replied, before hanging up.

D-Red pulled up on the side of him in a cranberry Aston Martin. Calvin rolled his window down. D-Red passed him a black duffel bag full of heroin.

"Go put that up. I gotta make moves," D-Red said.

"I'll get up with you later, Calvin replied, before tossing the bag on the passenger's seat.

Boony and One Eye Ty sat parked in a jet black Nissan Maxima with dirty dark tinted windows. They were two wild-ass young boys from Sands who made a living off of robberies.

"Yo, Boony, you saw that shit?" One Eye Ty asked, with a serious look on his face.

"That nigga, D-Red, just passed Calvin a bag. It got to be some work in there."

"Follow that nigga."

Calvin drove down the Ave. It was late night and the streets were dead. Besides a couple of fiends loitering on street corners, and hustlers getting money inside hallways, the streets were dead. Calvin had AZ *Pieces of a Black Man* playing real low on the CD deck, and a blunt of purple haze burning, as he headed to his stash house to drop off the work.

As he drove down Blue Hills Ave., he noticed a black Nissan Maxima tailing him. Calvin turned down Tower Ave. When the Nissan Maxima turned down Tower Ave., Calvin grabbed a chrome-and-black .40 cal. from out his glove box, turned off his headlights, and stomped on the gas.

The Audi A8's tires kicked up dust, as Calvin sped through the hood. The Nissan Maxima tried to keep up, but it was no match for the Audi A8. When Calvin got to Garden Street, he parked in back of the brick buildings on the bush and jumped out with the duffel bag full of drugs and his gun in-hand.

He hid in the darkness of the buildings with his gun in-hand, patiently waiting for the jouk boys to pull up. But they never did. Calvin called Trinicia's phone.

"Hello?" Trinicia said.

"Open the backdoor. I'm outside," Calvin said.

20

*   *   *

One Eye Ty sat in the passenger's seat with the ill grill on his face. Boony had blew the jouks, and One Eye Ty was feeling some type of way.

"How you let that nigga get away?" One Eye Ty asked.

"That Audi got balls. We need a faster whip," Boony replied.

One Eye Ty shook his head, as he thought about all the dope he missed out on.

*   *   *

D-Red pulled up on the block early morning. He had a jump off name Keosha in the passenger's seat and 50 Cent bumping in his whip. Monito was standing in front of the building running sales for Calvin. D-Red rolled his window down.

"Monito, where's Calvin?" D-Red asked.

"He's in the hallway, boss. I'll go get him," Monito replied.

Calvin walked out of the building dressed in all black. He had a serious look on his face, and D-Red could tell something was wrong with his boy.

"Calvin, what's good?" D-Red asked.

"Niggas tried to catch me slipping last night," Calvin replied.

"Word; who?"

"I don't know. After you dropped off the work last night, I was headed to the stash house. But I peeped niggas in a black Maxima following me. I took them on

21

a chase and lost them before going to Trinicia's crib for the night."

"So you still got the work?"

"Hell yeah, I ain't letting nobody take shit from me."

"I'm gone try to find out who got a black Maxima in the hood. Niggas is on the bullshit in the hood," D-Red indicated.

"You gotta stay on point."

"Most definitely."

Chapter 5

Mr. Ray Black sat in his office at CT Records looking at a magazine article on one of his artists named Politics. The headline read "Politics Caught Up in a Club Brawl". Politics and his entourage had beat up a 24-year-old man who had told Politics to suck his dick.

A verbal altercation sparked a fist fight between both crews and their entourage. The footage had been aired on all of the hip-hop sites, and television stations. Politics was a large artist in the rap industry, and a stunt like this could destroy his career. Mr. Ray Black buzzed his assistant, Daphny.

"Yes, Mr. Ray Black?"

"Where is Politics?"

"He just walked in the building," Daphny informed him.

"Tell him I need to see him."

"Will do, sir."

When Politics walked into Mr. Ray Black's office, he had a grin on his face with a cool demeanor, as he walked up to his desk.

"Mr. Ray Black, what's good?" Politics asked.

"What's wrong with you, Politics? You fighting cats in clubs now; what are you trying to do, throw ya career down the drain?" Mr. Ray Black asked.

"Mr. Ray Black, with all due respect, I can't be having these niggas out here thinking they can disrespect me! I got a street rep to uphold. So I keep it gangster 365 days a year, and seven days a week. Ya dig?" Politics asked.

Mr. Ray Black shook his head, as he listened to Politics try to justify his actions. As Politics told his side of the story, the only thing running through Mr. Ray Black's mind was hooking up with Melony. She was fine as hell and just the type of woman he could see his self wifing up.

*   *   *

The basketball courts in Waverly Park was packed on a Saturday afternoon. Everybody was outside parlaying and doing them. Weed smoke could be smelled in the air strong, and ladies were out in abundance. D-Red and Calvin stepped on the scene.

Tyreik and his crew of goons were in the park, as well. D-Red and Calvin walked over. They got pounds and hugs.

"Tyreik, what's good?" D-Red asked.

"Ain't shit, out here maintaining, trying to come up."

"That's right."

"The fiends be going crazy for that, Mo Money. I got the project banging right now," Tyreik said.

"I told you that shit was gone move."

"I need 10 stacks," Tyreik said, as he passed D-Red $2,500.

D-Red gave Tyreik a small brown paper bag which contained the 10 stacks of dope. After they handled business, D-Red and Calvin left the park. They never noticed One Eye Ty and Boony watching them from a distance with envious stares.

*　　*　　*

Unique, Melony, and Candy hung out at Unique's condo, watching *These Evil Streets* and smoking weed, while talking about the latest gossip in the hood.

"Y'all hear about Rochelle?" Melony asked.

"Nah, what happened?" Candy asked, curiously.

"She got locked up the other day. The Feds ran up in her crib and found a kilo of cocaine. When she wouldn't tell them whose drugs it was, they locked her up."

"Devin didn't own up to the drugs?"

"They said he wasn't there, and his name ain't on the lease. So technically, unless she cooperate, Rochelle is hit," Melony explained.

"If he let that girl go down for his drugs, he's a real piece of shit," Candy said.

"I agree," Melony replied.

The realization that her crib could be next began to dawn on Unique, and she became nervous. D-Red wasn't your average corner boy. And the amount of drugs he ran through on a daily basis could easily land both of them behind bars for life.

*　　*　　*

D-Red stood in the hallway on Belden Street, counting cash, when his cell phone started ringing.

"Hello?" D-Red said.

"I need to talk to you," Unique replied.

"Is everything all right?"

"No, it's not all right. Where are you?"

25

"On the block, where you at?" D-Red answered.

"Around the corner, I'm pulling up now."

D-Red came outside when Unique pulled up in her Benz CLK. He jumped in the passenger's seat and looked at Unique.

"What's going on, baby?"

"You gotta get this shit out of my house!" Unique said, as she tossed D-Red a duffel bag full of guns and heroin.

"Unique, what the fuck is wrong with you pulling up on this hot-ass block with all this shit?" D-Red asked, angrily.

"You gotta put this shit somewhere else! I'm not going to jail for life behind yo ass."

"Unique, what are you talking about?"

"The Feds rushed Rochelle's crib the other night and locked her up for a kilo of cocaine that Devin had stashed in her house. And on top of all that, he let her go down for it," Unique informed him.

"Baby, first of all, I'm a man. And I would never let you go to prison for my shit. It's just not in me. And second of all, Devin was an idiot. He served a Federal Agent for about six months before they finally locked him up."

Unique wiped the tears from her face, as she began to calm down.

"I would still sleep a lot better if you put this stuff somewhere else."

"All right, I got you," D-Red said, before giving Unique a kiss on the lips and hopping out of the whip with the duffel bag full of drugs.

He walked into the building and stashed the work in one of his apartments on the block. A black pit bull with a white patch on his chest walked up to D-Red and began to jump on him, excitedly.

"Big Boy, what's up?" D-Red asked the dog, as he petted him.

D-Red placed the duffel bag on the kitchen table before grabbing some dog food and placing it in Big Boy's bowl. D-Red called up a few of his workers to distribute the dope. He couldn't risk leaving that much dope on the block, unattended.

Being on the level he was on in the game, he had no room for slipups. He had to stay 10 steps ahead of all of his enemies. When Calvin arrived at the apartment, he was given the bulk of the heroin to distribute.

"We gotta put this shit on the streets. Double up on all our workers' packages," D-Red said.

"Why? What's up?" Calvin asked.

"I gotta find a new stash house for the dope. But right now, we can't risk leaving it on the block."

"All right, I'll take care of it."

Chapter 6

Candy and Jerome kissed passionately in Candy's living room. Jerome's hands traveled all over her body, starting with her large breasts. She moaned out loudly, as he played with her nipples. Candy was hot, wet, and ready to take it to the next level.

Jerome lifted her onto the kitchen counter, spread her legs apart, and put his face in between her thighs. The skirt she was wearing gave him easy access. He slid her panties to the side and began to suck on her clit, going from side-to-side with his tongue, getting her wetter and wetter by the second.

"Oh, yes, baby! Right there," Candy yelled, as she held the back of his head.

Jerome continued to please her orally until she couldn't take anymore. Her juices began to flow, as she reached an orgasm. Jerome came up for air. He kissed on her luscious lips, while penetrating her.

"Oh!" Candy moaned, as he slid into her love box.

She began to scratch up his back, as he filled her up with his love muscle. Jerome hit her with long and deep strokes, as she panted and moaned out his name. They switched positions. Jerome began to hit her doggy style.

Candy's ass was bounding with every stroke, like a bowl of Jell-o on the move; when Jerome couldn't hold back any longer, he skeeted off into the Rough Rider condom.

"Ah, shit, baby, I'm cumming!" Jerome yelled.

"I'm cumming with you, daddy," Candy replied, in a sexy voice, making him cum harder.

They took a hot and steamy shower together to wash off the sex before watching *Think Like a Man* on DVD.

*   *   *

Mr. Ray Black sat in his mansion out in Norwich, Connecticut. He had his computer open. Realrap.com was interviewing his artist, Political.

"Political, what's going on, my man," Antoine, the host of the show, asked.

"Man, you know me, man. I'm doing me, as usual. I got my new album, *Politics As Usual* about to drop December 7th. And I'm on my grind hard body."

"That's what's up. But you were recently caught up in a club brawl. Do you mind elaborating on that?"

"It ain't too much to elaborate on. Some clown-ass nigga came out his mouth sideways. So I had to crush him; plain and simple as that," Political explained.

"We got footage that says different," Antoine replied.

The crowd began to yell oohs and ahs.

"What footage?" Political asked.

"Play the tape," Antoine said, with a smile on his face.

The tape began to play. Political could be seen exchanging words with a man named Reemo. Reemo hooked off on Political, catching him in the jaw. Political fell up against the bar. Political's entourage rushed Reemo and began to rain blows on the man.

29

Political shook off the blow and joined in on the fight. They kicked and stomped Reemo out until his crew joined in. A big brawl popped off in the club. Bottles and chairs were flying everywhere, and Political was running and ducking for cover behind his crew.

When the audience finished watching the footage, they were in shock. If they hadn't seen it with their own eyes, they would have never believed Political was running behind his crew like a little bitch. Political was boiling, while sitting on the couch at realrap.com.

"Man, where you get this tape? This shit is fake! Man, that ain't me," Political said, seriously.

"It looks like you to me," Antoine replied, as he looked at the footage.

Political snuffed Antoine out of his seat.

"Nigga, what you trying to play me!" Political yelled, before Security hauled him off the show.

The crowd looked on in shock, as Political was dragged off the stage. Derek, Antoine's Security Guard, helped Antoine off the floor.

"I'm okay, people. We gotta go to a commercial break and we will be right back with more realrap.com," Antoine said, before the show went to commercial.

Mr. Ray Black shook his head in disappointment, as he watched Political dig his self a deeper grave in the rap industry. Antoine was a highly respected man in the music business, and always showed love to artists on the come-up.

His hip-hop show was one of the largest rap shows watched online. And Political had just blown that plug for his self. Mr. Ray Black dialed Antoine's number

ASAP to try to patch things up between him and his artist. But his phone was going straight to voicemail.

Chapter 7

Unique, Melony, and Candy sat up in Flava's Beauty Salon on Friday afternoon. The shop was packed, and gossip was in the air heavy.

"Girl, did y'all catch realrap.com last night?" Twanetta asked.

"Nah, who was up there?" Unique asked.

"That fine-ass rapper, Political."

"I don't really like his music," Melony added, with a distasteful look on her face.

"Girl, he showed his ass last night, though. You know how Antoine be putting niggas on blast on his show?"

"Yeah."

"He tried that shit with Political and got knocked out," Twanetta said.

"Get out of here."

"I'm dead serious. I ain't lying."

"Wow," Unique gasped.

"But that ain't the half of it, though. Come to find out some nigga named Reemo knocked Political out. The only thing that saved him was his homeboys coming to help him. Otherwise, that boy would have beat his ass," Twanetta said.

"All that gangster talk he be rapping about, and he can't even fight," Unique said.

"Girl, that's the new thing to do these days. These niggas is lying in 80 percent of their rhymes," Melony added.

The women in the shop began to laugh, as they continued to gossip about all the drama going on in the hood.

*   *   *

Political knocking Antoine out on realrap.com was the talk of the town. Everybody had an opinion about the situation. And Lil Crimey and his crew of Bloods were no different.

"Yo, Blood, that nigga, Antoine, got stretched the fuck out on live TV, Five. The nigga Political just laid him," Red Rum said, with a smile on his face.

"Word to Blood, Political is a bitch. Why he ain't do that to that nigga, Reemo, when he put hands on him?" Lil Crimey asked.

"Man, they beat blood out that nigga, Reemo. What you talking about, Five?" Red Rum replied.

"Yeah, after his mans had to jump the nigga. Political ain't built like that. He be fronting for TV for real. Don't let me catch him in the hood. I'm gone see if he really bout that."

"Man, I fucks with Political. He got some hot shit. Don't hate on the nigga, Blood."

"Man, fuck that nigga. I catch him out here, he food, Blood," Lil Crimey warned.

Red Rum started smiling, as he listened to Lil Crimey express his hatred for the rapper.

"Yo, what's up with Tori and her sister, Carmen? I'm trying to get some pussy. Fuck them rap niggas," Real Deal said, while twisting up a Dutch Master filled with Kush.

"Call them bitches up, Blood," Lil Crimey replied, while thinking about Carmen's big-ass titties.

*   *   *

Political sat in his $400,000 home out in Glastonbury, in a gated community, watching *Hip Hop News* with his wife, Kimberly. Since the altercation with Antoine, they had been slaying him on all the hip-hop sites. He turned the volume up on the television when Runny Ran, the news anchor, started talking about him.

"Rap Artist, Political, assaulted Antoine, the host of realrap.com, yesterday, when he put him on blast about a club brawl in which he was involved in. If you look at the footage here, you can see Political being knocked out by a kid named Remo.

"The only thing that stopped him from being thrashed real badly by the boy was his Security, which he calls his entourage. Now, Hobbs, I'm from the old school. And back in my day, you had to prove you were really gangster if you wanted street rep.

"Nowadays, these rappers pick up a mike and just be faking. What's your input on this situation?" Runny Ran asked.

"Well, Runny Ran, I think the kid, Political, knows how to choose his battles well. He would have never came to *Hip Hop News* and pulled a stunt like that, because they would have been having to drag him up off the floor when I was done with him.

"But that's neither here nor there. I don't like what he did to Antoine. And to keep it 100 with you, I think Antoine deserves an apology," Hobbs replied.

34

"I agree. Political, if you're listening, man up and do the right thing. Because if you don't, your career's going down the toilet," Runny Ran said, before Political cut the television off and sucked his teeth.

"Bay, don't pay them no mind. They just talking. You're the hottest rapper in Connecticut right now," Kimberly said, trying to boost her man's ego.

"Yeah, but this thing is really making me look bad in the eyes of the public. You should see the shit people been writing about me on Twitter and Facebook," Political replied, while getting frustrated.

"So, what are you going to do?"

"I don't know yet," Political replied.

"Listen to what your heart says," Kimberly added, before leaving her man to his thoughts.

*   *   *

Mr. Ray Black dialed Antoine's number once again, trying to reach him. He had been calling him all day, but had yet to be successful. The phone rung about six times before someone picked up the phone.

"Hello," Mr. Ray Black said.

The other person on the other end didn't reply.

"Antoine, is that you, man? Look, I'm real sorry about what happened between you and my artist, Political. If I was there, I would have never let it go down like that. Political is real hot-headed. But I know he feels fucked about what he did to you," Mr. Ray Black said.

"How do you know? Did he tell you that?" Antoine asked, finally replying.

"No, but I know he is. Political is the type of guy who does things sometimes without thinking."

"That still doesn't make it right."

"I know, and I hope we can work this thing out," Mr. Ray Black stated.

"Anything can be worked out, for a price," Antoine replied, while smiling on the other end of the phone.

"How much?"

"A hundred thousand dollars and a complimentary suite at your new hotel for a full year."

"Done, anything else?" Mr. Ray Black replied.

"And an apology on my show from Political."

"I got you."

Mr. Ray Black hung up the phone feeling a whole lot better. Now that he had patched things up with Antoine, his only problem left was convincing his artist, Political, that apologizing was the right thing to do. Political was a platinum-selling artist.

And he couldn't risk losing all the cash he had invested in him. He looked at the $100,000 investment as security for his money he invested in Political. He would recoup it back off album sales before Political would see another dime. So it was nothing to him.

Chapter 8

Carmen moaned out in pleasure, as she rode Lil Crimey in the driver's seat of a Chevy Lumina van. Her sister, Tori, was in the back of the van getting her back blown out by Real Deal, while she sucked Red Rum off. A wild sex episode was popping off.

And Lil Crimey and his Blood crew were loving it. Red Rum was the first one to bust off. Tori didn't spill a drop of his juices, and would have kept going if he didn't push her face away. She had made him tap out. But Real Deal and Lil Crimey were still going at it.

"Fuck this pussy, Blood!" Tori moaned, as Real Deal smacked on her ass cheeks and hit it doggy style.

Her box was so wet, Real Deal felt like he wasn't even wearing a condom. Tori began to throw her ass back on him, making Real Deal skeet off.

"Ah, shit, baby, you got a nigga cumming!" Real Deal yelled.

Lil Crimey squeezed on Carmen's large breasts, as she continued to ride his dick. Her breast were soft as cotton, and had Lil Crimey on the verge of busting off. Carmen began to speak in Spanish, as she nibbled on his right ear.

The sound of her sexy voice and mouth on his ear made Lil Crimey bust off into her sugar walls. He got in a few more pumps, as he held her close to him.

"Damn, this pussy's good!" Lil Crimey said, as he squeezed on her big round ass.

"This is all yours, Papi, anytime you want it," Carmen replied, as she fixed her miniskirt.

37

*   *   *

Political was sitting in his black-on-black Aston
Martin, watching his newest video on BET, when he got
a call on his phone from Mr. Ray Black. Political picked
up after the second ring.

"Hello?" Political said.

"We need to talk."

"I'll be at your office in an hour."

The phone went dead in Political's ear. He could
tell Mr. Ray Black was pissed about the situation
between him and Antoine. Political sighed, before
pulling away from the curb. He knew Mr. Ray Black
would be calling him sooner or later to discuss all the
bullshit he was getting his self caught up in.

*   *   *

D-Red and Calvin met up with Tyreik in the back
of Chappelle Gardens. He came out of the building
dressed in all black, with a book bag in his hand. When
he jumped in the backseat of the Lexus truck they were
driving, he gave Calvin and D-Red dap.

"What up, my nigga? You black down like you
ready to go to war," D-Red said, jokingly.

"Niggas from the other side got it fucked up. They
clapped one of my little homies last night," Tyreik
replied.

"I'm sorry to hear that."

"Shit about to get real ugly out here. Let me get
30 stacks," Tyreik said, as he passed D-Red two knots of
money, wrapped in rubber bands.

D-Red cuffed the money in his inside pocket and passed Tyreik the dope.

"Yo, hit my phone if you need me," D-Red said, before giving Tyreik dap.

"All right," Tyreik replied, as he jumped out of the truck.

D-Red looked at Calvin and shook his head.

"Niggas out here letting the beef cook hard in the streets," D-Red said.

"Survival of the fittest."

"Man, fuck all that beefing shit. I'm trying to get money."

"To each his own."

Chapter 9

Unique, Melony, and Candy stood by the bar at Mr. Ray Black's new club. A track by Remy Martin blasted through the speakers. Mr. Ray Black was nowhere to be found, but he had sent Melony invitations to attend his new club for free.

She had yet to give him her address. So he mailed them to her job, Flava's Beauty Salon. The club was an upscale club and had a guest list. If you weren't on it, you weren't getting in, unless you were with somebody on the guest list.

The spot was that exclusive. Some of the hottest entertainers, sports figures, business moguls, and exotic women were all in the building.

"This club is hot. Ain't that Mike Charles over there in the VIP section?" Melony asked.

"Yeah, that's his fine ass. I love his music," Unique replied, as she admired him from across the room.

Mike Charles noticed her checking him out. He smiled and she smiled back. When an exotic Jamaican-and-Asian model sat down next to Mike Charles and wrapped her arm around his waist, Unique frowned her face up in disappointment. Melony and Candy started laughing.

"Girl, you need to quit flirting with that boy. You got a whole man at home waiting for you," Melony said.

"Yeah, but it's just something about him that gets my panties moist."

"Girl, you a freak."

Unique smiled, as she took a sip from her drink. JC walked over with a smile on his face.

"What's up, ladies?" JC asked.

"Hey, JC," the ladies replied in unison.

"Mr. Ray Black's not going to be able to make it out to the club tonight. But he told me to make sure y'all had a good time tonight. Everything is on the house tonight. I got a table set up for y'all in the VIP area, and bottles of the finest champagne lined up," JC said.

"Did he say why he wouldn't be able to make it?" Melony asked.

"No, he didn't say. But he told me to tell you that your on his mind and he will call soon."

Melony blushed just from hearing those words.

"I'll show you ladies to your table."

*   *   *

When Political walked into CT Records, Mr. Ray Black's assistant was sitting at the front desk.

"Is Mr. Ray Black in yet?" Political asked.

"He's in his office. He's expecting you," the secretary replied.

When Political walked into Mr. Ray Black's office, he had footage of Political assaulting Antoine on his big screen television. Political's whole facial expression changed to a sad look, when he saw the tape playing.

"Look, I already know what you gone say, Mr. Ray Black. I fucked up and I'm willing to do whatever I gotta do to make things right," Political said.

"Good, because the first thing you gone do is apologize to Antoine on his show."

41

"After what I did, I doubt if I'll ever be able to step foot on his show again."

"I worked everything out. You just do your part and start thinking before you make dumb decisions like you did the other day. You got a lot to lose, Political. Right now you're a platinum-selling artist. So your every move is viewed by the public. You got an image to uphold. So don't fuck that up."

"I got you," Political stated.

"Go get some rest. You got a lot of work to do in the morning."

"So when am I scheduled to go on the show?"

"I'll call and give you all the details," Mr. Ray Black informed him.

"All right."

Political gave Mr. Ray Black dap before walking out the door. Mr. Ray Black grabbed his phone from out his drawer and looked at the screen. He had six missed calls. Three of them were from Melony, and the other three were business-related.

Mr. Ray Black called Melony back ASAP. She had been on his mind all day, but business had to come before pleasure. It was a model he lived by for years, and was one of the reasons he was so successful.

*   *   *

Melony had just came in from the club and was tipsy from all the champagne she had consumed. As she stepped into her living room, her cell phone started ringing.

"Hello?" Melony said.

42

"What's up? What you doing?" Mr. Ray Black asked.

"I just left your club. What happened to you tonight?"

"I had to handle some business with one of my artists."

"Where are you now?" Melony inquired.

"At my office."

"When will I see you again?"

"I was on my way out the door now. Can I see you tonight?" Mr. Ray Black queried, hopeful.

"Meet me at the Sheraton Hotel."

"I'm on my way now."

"Okay, baby."

Mr. Ray Black smiled, as he hung up the phone.

Chapter 10

Silk and Ghetto cruised down Capen Street in a black Oldsmobile Delta '88. Meek Mills bumped through the speakers, as Ghetto analyzed all the hustlers posted up on the block. When he spotted his victim, he tapped his man, Silk, on the arm.

"Silk, pull up on that nigga, Leo," Ghetto said, calmly.

Silk dipped on the side of Leo like he was the Police. Ghetto had a .50 caliber handgun in his hand, as he rolled the window down.

"Leo, let me holla at you, playboy," Ghetto said.

Leo's whole facial expression changed to a shocked look, when he noticed who was in the car.

"What up, baby?" Leo asked, as he walked up to the car.

"You got that for me?" Ghetto asked.

"You gotta give me a minute, Ghetto. Shit been mad slow out here all week."

"Leo, don't fucking play with me! Run mine's before I put some hot slugs in ya chest."

"Come on, Ghetto, you ain't gotta take it there," Leo said, as he dug in his pocket and pulled out a wad of cash.

Ghetto grabbed the cash from his hand, aggressively.

"Stop playing with me, Leo. You gone make me do you dirty out here! Have my bread the same time next week."

Silk turned up Meek Mills before pulling off. Leo cursed his self for letting Silk and Ghetto catch him slipping. He had been doing a good job of ducking them for the past couple days. But he knew it would only be a matter of time before they bumped heads again.

Silk and Ghetto had been extorting Leo for about a year. He was paying them weekly, but had began to start ducking them about a month ago. Ghetto had pistol-whipped Leo in his hallway before, when he took three weeks to pay him.

Ghetto had Leo on some shook shit. But Leo still played games whenever he could get away with it. Leo sold a lot of cocaine in the hood. So the wolves were on his ass for that paper.

*   *   *

When Melony let Mr. Ray Black into her hotel room, she was dressed in a red silk negligee.

"You look amazing," Mr. Ray Black said, as he wrapped his arms around her waist and held her close to him.

"Thank you," Melony replied, with a seductive smile on her face.

Mr. Ray Black got lost in her eyes, before they began to kiss passionately. Melony slid her hand into his pants and began to stroke him off. She had him about to bust out of his jeans. Melony unzipped his pants, dropped down to her knees, and began to suck him off.

Mr. Ray Black's eyes rolled to the back of his head, as she sucked him off. His legs began to buckle, as she sucked the life out of him. When he couldn't hold back any longer, he came all on her tonsils. Melony swallowed every drop of his babies. As Mr. Ray Black climaxed, his secretary walked in his office, taking him out of his thoughts.

"Mr. Ray Black, Political just arrived," Mona said.

"Have him wait for me in the waiting room. I'll call for him when I'm ready."

"Okay, sir."

"And bring me one of my suits out of the backroom. I'll be in the shower," Mr. Ray Black instructed her.

"Yes, sir."

Mr. Ray Black had it bad for Melony and had to have her. He often dreamed about her, and hadn't even had the pleasure of smelling her panties yet.

Chapter 11

Dip Set bumped through Lil Crimey's rental, as he pulled up on Elmer Street. Reek was posted up in front of the corner store, getting money. Lil Crimey pulled on the side of him.

"What up, Blood? Where the bud at?" Lil Crimey asked.

"What you need, Five?" Reek asked.

"Let me get two for 25," Lil Crimey said, as he passed Reek $25.

Reek dropped two $15 bags of piff in Lil Crimey's hand.

"This fire, Blood?" Lil Crimey asked.

"That's it? That's dope right there, bra!"

Lil Crimey smelled the weed and nodded his head in approval.

"Yeah, this is it right here, Blood. Let me get two more bags," Lil Crimey said, as he passed Reek some more bills balled up.

Reek passed Lil Crimey the bud. Lil Crimey pulled off. Reek counted the cash and gritted his teeth when he realized it was only $6. He called Lil Crimey's phone, but it went straight to voicemail. He knew Lil Crimey was a grimy little nigga.

But he never thought he would snake him, based on the fact that they were both Bloods. But Lil Crimey was a piece of shit and lived off crutball principles.

* * *

D-Red sat in his brand-new Range Rover truck, watching *Paid in Full*, while smoking on a blunt of purple haze. His phone had been ringing all night with dope sales, and he was getting it. Calvin played the passenger's seat with a chrome-and-black .45 automatic on his lap, just in case the jouk boys tried to act up late night.

I'm gone have to see the connect in a minute. I'm down to about 7 ounces of raw," D-Red said, as he counted the cash.

"I got about the same," Calvin replied.

"Bring me whatever cash you got. I'm trying to copp heavy."

"I'll have it to you by the morning."

D-Red pulled up in back of Calvin's S-550 Benz. Calvin gave him dap before jumping out of the truck.

"What you about to get into?" Calvin asked.

"I'm about to go check Daphny."

"You still smashing that? You better fall back before Unique kick yo ass."

D-Red started laughing.

"I'll be all right. Daphny ain't the type of chick to kiss and tell."

"Yeah, all right," Calvin replied, before walking away form the truck.

D-Red called Daphny up ASAP. Daphny rolled over in her bed in nothing but a t-shirt and panties when she heard her phone ringing. She answered after the third ring in a sleepy voice.

"Hello?" Daphny said.

"What's up, baby? What you doing?" D-Red asked.

48

"I'm in the bed sleeping. What happened to you? You were supposed to come through hours ago."

"I was chilling with my boy, Calvin, and lost track of time."

"So why you calling me this late?" Daphny asked, groggy.

"Because I'm trying to come through."

"I don't know, D-Red. It's kinda late."

"Come on, baby. Let a nigga spend some time with you. I'll make it worth ya while," D-Red begged.

"Oh, yeah, and how's that?"

"You know that new Prada bag you been asking me for?"

"Yeah," Daphny said, excitedly.

"I got that for you this morning."

"You lying."

"Come on, now, Daphny. Why would I lie to you, girl? You know I'm caked up to the ceiling. That's something light," D-Red bragged.

"Boy, hurry up before I go back to sleep."

"Say no more."

D-Red put the Range Rover in drive and sped to her crib before she could change her mind. He grabbed the new Prada bag that he planned on giving to Unique from out the trunk and walked upstairs with it in-hand. As he walked up the steps, he saw Militant One in the hallway smoking dust.

"D-Red, what up, Kik? You got work?" Militant One asked.

"Yeah, what's good?"

"Let me get two stacks."

Militant One passed D-Red $500. D-Red handed him two stacks of dope.

"Militant One, you need to leave them black bags alone, my nigga. That ain't a good look."

"This is how I escape my reality, homey. Sometimes I gotta get lost in the matrix."

D-Red cracked a smile before knocking on Daphny's door. He knew Militant One was crazy, and the PCP didn't make his state of mind any better. When Daphny came to the door in nothing but her t-shirt and panties, D-Red's dick got rock hard quick. He bit down on his bottom lip with lust in his eyes, as he stared her up and down.

"Damn, girl, you looking sexy as shit right now."

Daphny smiled.

"Where my bag at?" Daphny asked, with her hand out.

D-Red handed her the Prada bag.

"Damn, ma, that's all I'm good for?"

Daphny walked up to him and slid her small hand into his Gucci sweatpants.

"That's not all you good for, daddy," Daphny replied, as she began to fondle him.

"Damn, that feels good," D-Red said, as he let Daphny work her magic.

Chapter 12

After Mr. Ray Black's talk with Political, he had convinced him that apologizing to Antoine was the right thing to do. It had taken some convincing, but Political finally got it through his head. Political had less than an hour before he would appear on the show. And he was kinda nervous. Political's wife, Kimberly, walked up behind her man and wrapped her arms around his waist.

"Baby, relax. Everything is going to be fine," Kimberly assured her man.

"I hope so."

*   *   *

Lil Crimey and his Blood gang hung out at Red Rum's crib on Judson Street, smoking bud, Arizona, and drinking Seagram's gin. They were twisted, while watching realrap.com.

"What's up, world? We got a hot new show for y'all today. R&B Artist Mike Charles is in the building today," Antoine said.

The crowd began to cheer loudly.

"We also got the sexy rapstress, Mina-J, in the building."

The crowd got even hyper.

"Political will also be on the show today."

The crowd began to boo when they heard his name.

"let's be nice people, and see what he has to say before we get upset," Antoine said, calming the crowd.

Lil Crimey shook his head.

"See, this the shit I'm talking about, Blood! Now this nigga wanna come back to the show and talk shit out. Real gangsters don't do that. I'm trying to chalk shit out," Lil Crimey replied, before taking a pull off of his blunt.

"You shoulda been a rapper," Red Rum replied.

"That shit did sound hard, right, Blood?" Lil Crimey asked, with a smile on his face.

"Yo, chill, let me hear what this nigga got to say," Real Deal said, as he turned up the volume on the computer.

Political walked on the stage and shook hands with Antoine.

"First off, Antoine, I want to apologize for putting my hands on you, homey. What I did was real fucked up and I gotta live with the fact that I assaulted my brother on live TV," Political said, seriously.

The crowd began to clap. They calmed down, as Antoine began to speak.

"Brother, I know what you saying right now here on my show took a lot for you to say. It takes a lot to be the bigger man and admit when you're wrong. So, brother, I accept your apology," Antoine said.

Both men stood up and embraced in a brotherly hug. The crowd began to clap loudly. Lil Crimey sucked his teeth.

"Man, them niggas is bitch-made," Lil Crimey said, as he watched them peace up their beef.

"Nah, man, that was some real shit. Sometimes you gotta be the bigger man, Blood. He ain't do nothing wrong," Red Rum said, seriously.

"I leave all that kissing and making up to my women friend," Lil Crimey replied, with a smirk on his face.

"You a funny nigga, Blood," Real Deal replied, before they all started laughing.

Chapter 13

The best of G-Unit bumped through the speakers inside of Tyreik's rental, as he pulled up in the back of Holly Wood. Hustlers were posted up in back of the bricks, getting money and shooting dice, when he jumped out of his rental with the mean mug on his face.

"What's up, Tyreik? You all right, Blood?" Low Life asked.

"Niggas was just busting at me on Garden. Them little niggas from the Deuce almost caught me slipping," Tyreik replied.

"What they was in, Blood?"

"A white Maxima with out-of-state plates."

"Word to Blood, I saw that same Max come through the projects last night. I was in the building, so I ain't pay it too much attention. But come to think about it now, that definitely was them same niggas."

"So what y'all trying to do?" Scumbag asked.

"We going through there, Blood," Lil Crimey said, with no hesitation.

Before they could all agree, shots popped off in their direction, making them run for cover. Tyreik ran behind his rental and pulled out a .50 caliber handgun from out of his waistband and began busting at two men dressed in all black with bandanas over their faces and guns in their hands. Lil Crimey pulled out a TEC-9 equipped with an extended clip.

Boc! Boc! Boc! Boc! Boc! Boom! Boom!

"Ah!" the taller masked man yelled, as a slug tore through his kneecap, making him fall to the floor.

The .45 auto he was clutching fell to the concrete. His partner in crime took off on foot, leaving his comrade for dead. Bullets whizzed past his head, as he ran for his life. When he got to Charlotte Street, he jumped in the passenger's seat of the white Nissan Maxima.

"Pull off!" Ron-Ron yelled to the driver.

"Kik, where is Links?" Prada asked.

"He didn't make it," Ron-Ron replied.

Boc! Boc! Boc!

Bullets crashed through the back window of the Nissan Maxima. Prada peeled off recklessly. Low Life stood in the middle of the street, busting at the fleeing Maxima. Links tried to crawl to his banger that laid on the ground a few feet away from him. Lil Crimey stomped on his hand, crushing his fingers.

"Ah, shit!" Links cried out in pain.

"What the fuck you was gone do with this, Blood?" Lil Crimey asked, as he picked the gun up from the ground and pointed it at the man's face.

"Kill yo bitch ass!" Links replied, angrily.

"Tough talk for a man who's about to die," Lil Crimey replied, as he snatched the black bandana from the man's face.

Lil Crimey began to smile excitedly when he realized who his victim was.

"Links, I been waiting a long time to put you in the ground with ya niggas. You got any last words before I slump you, Blood?"

"I'll see yo bitch ass in hell, nigga! This war ain't never gone stop! A.V.E. Finest, bitch!" Links yelled.

Boc! Boc! Boc! Boc! Boc!

Bullets ripped into Links' face, head, and neck, making blood spray all over the pavement. Lil Crimey and his Blood crew walked away casually, leaving Links in a pool of blood with his thoughts on the curb.

*   *   *

Prada jacked Ron-Ron up against a fence on Edgewood Street when they bailed out of the rental.

"You let Links get killed! I should murk yo bitch ass right now!" Prada said, as he pulled out a Glock .40 and put it to Ron-Ron's forehead. Block took Ron-Ron's gun out of his waistband.

"Come on, Kik. It wasn't my fault," Ron-Ron said, with tears in his eyes.

"Fuck you mean it wasn't your fault? You left the little homey for dead!"

"It wasn't even like that. Them niggas almost killed me. It was nothing I could do."

Prada began to pistol-whip Ron-Ron viciously. Block dug in his pockets, taking his money and drugs.

"Don't let me catch you out here no more! Fuck outta here, Fam! You lucky I ain't body yo ass out here!"

Ron-Ron ran up the block, damn near falling to the ground trying to get away from Prada. He knew Prada's words were so sincere, and he didn't want no problems. Prada and his homies were heated. Ron-Ron had gotten Links killed, and nobody knew the real story but Ron-Ron and the Bloods who had killed him. As Prada and his homies walked into the blue house on Edgewood, his cell phone started ringing.

56

"Hello?" Prada said.

"What's popping, Blood?" Lil Crimey asked.

"Who's this?" Prada asked.

"We just caught ya man, Links, slipping in the pjs. He's no longer with us," Lil Crimey said, before he started laughing.

"I'm gone kill all you niggas!" Prada said, angrily.

"Nah, what you need to do is kill that soft-ass nigga who left ya man for dead. He's a real bitch. But ya man, Links, he went out like a gee before I blew half his face off!"

"I'm coming for you, niggas! Don't sleep, because I'm coming!" Prada yelled into the phone.

"You better come heavy!" Lil Crimey replied, before hanging up on Prada.

Chapter 14

Political apologizing on realrap.com was the topic of discussion. Everybody had their own views on the whole situation. Political was in the crib watching *Hip Hop News* when they started talking about him.

"Runny Ran, what do you think about Political apologizing to Antoine after knocking him out on live TV?" Hobbs asked.

"I think that was the smartest thing he could have done, due to the situation," Runny Ran replied.

"So you don't think this whole thing was a publicity stunt to boost album sales on his new album that's getting ready to drop?"

"If it was, it definitely was a foolish one that almost destroyed his career," Runny Ran said.

"A lot of people don't feel like his apology was genuine."

"At the end of the day, if you ask me, I don't think he's really sorry for what he did. But only he knows deep down in his heart."

Political began to flick through the hip-hop channels, and noticed they were talking about him on all of the hip-hop stations. Political jumped on his laptop and noticed all the positive Tweets he was getting on Twitter for apologizing to Antoine. Political smiled, as he continued to scroll through the Tweets.

*   *   *

D-Red walked into Carlos' bodega on the south end. As he walked to the back of the store, one of

Carlos' goons was leaning against a deep freezer with a sawed-off 12-shot Mossberg pump in his hand, and a mean mug on his grill.

The man never said much, but had a reputation for being a ruthless killer. He had killed for Carlos on many occasions and wouldn't hesitate to kill in a second, if his boss gave him the word. Deep down inside, Carlos didn't like blacks and only let them in his circle because they spent so much money with him.

"D-Red, what can I do for you?" Carlos asked, as he sat back at the round table.

"I need 10 kilos of raw."

Carlos smiled.

"Business has been good, I see."

"You could say that."

"You hungry?" Carlos questioned.

"Nah, I'm cool."

"Sit down and have a drink with me. It's always a pleasure doing business with you. Did you bring the money?"

D-Red dropped a large duffel bag full of cash in front of Carlos' foot. He began to speak in Spanish to a Puerto Rican woman in her late 40s. She grabbed the bag and disappeared into a room upstairs. Carlos went into a freezer and began to pull kilos of heroin wrapped in Saran wrap out of the freezer.

He stuffed them into a black book back and placed it by his foot. His wife came into the room with two plates of roast pork and rice, and beans. She placed a plate in front of D-Red and one in front of Carlos.

"Eat something, pai. It's not good to drink on an empty stomach," Carlos said.

59

D-Red reluctantly picked up the fork and began to eat. He knew Carlos would keep bugging him until he did. But Carlos' main concern wasn't D-Red eating. He was stalling the deal until all the cash was counted and accounted for. When D-Red finally got up out of there with the work, he met up with his man, Calvin, so they could cut, bag, and distribute the heroin throughout the city.

Chapter 15

Club 860 was popping on a Saturday night. Meek Mills was performing and the ladies were out in abundance.

"Yo, it's jumping in here tonight," Calvin said, as he popped a bottle of Ace of Spade.

"Word," D-Red replied, as he sipped on a cup of Grey Goose mixed with cranberry juice.

As they chilled by the bar, Daphny walked over to D-Red and began dancing. She was backing her ass up against him while his hands explored all over her body. The skin-tight silk miniskirt she was wearing left little to the imagination.

Calvin looked on with a disapproving look on his face, as D-Red played with fire out in public. He knew situations like these were bad for business. Unique knew too much and if she ever found out about D-Red's infidelity, she could destroy everything they worked so hard to build. Calvin whispered into D-Red's ear.

"Tighten up, homey. You know the streets is watching," Calvin said.

D-Red cracked a smile.

"Let them watch," D-Red replied, as he fondled Daphny's breasts.

*   *   *

Unique, Melony, and Candy stepped into Club 860. They all were looking right, and all eyes were on them, as they moved through the crowd. The lights were dim and weed smoke and liquor could be smelled in the air

61

heavy. As Unique and her girls got closer to the bar, they were stopped by Calvin.

"Hey, what's up, ladies? What y'all doing up in here?" Calvin asked, with a smile on his face.

"We came to see Meek Mills. Where my man at?" Unique asked, as she began to look around the club for D-Red.

"He's somewhere around here," Calvin replied, stalling for time.

As Unique continued to look around the club, D-Red crept up behind her and wrapped his arms around her waist. His Polo Sport cologne got her panties moist as soon as it invaded her nostrils.

"What's up, baby? When you get here?" D-Red asked.

"Me and my girls just got here."

"I got a table over in the VIP. You and ya girls can hang out with us," D-Red said.

"We can do that," Unique replied, as she began to follow her man to the VIP section.

She stopped dead in her tracks when she saw her little cousin, Daphny, sitting at the bar, drinking a Long Island iced tea.

"Daphny, what's up, girl? Who you here with?" Unique asked.

"By myself, what's going on, cuz?" Daphny asked, with a fake smile on her face, as she hugged her cousin.

"I'm chilling. You want to hang out with us in the VIP?"

"I don't want to intrude on you and ya friends."

"Girl, stop playing. You is family and you hanging out with us tonight," Unique insisted.

"If you insist."

Daphny followed them to the VIP area, where they partied, popped bottles, and watched Meek Mills perform. The only thing running through D-Red's head was finding a way to slide off to Daphny's crib for the night. Calvin's thoughts was totally different, though. He knew his homey's cheating ways could be the downfall of both of them.

Chapter 16

Detective Jennings and his partner, Detective Brenton, stood in the back of Chappelle Gardens staring at the man laying on the ground, lifeless. Different caliber shell casings, Dutch Master guts, and crushed glass was on the ground, as well. Detective Jennings walked over to Officer Camden.

"You mind giving us a rundown," Detective Jennings asked.

"Julius Crews aka Links was gunned down. He's a 28-year-old black male, who has had a few run-ins with the law, for grand theft auto and weapons possession."

"Do we have a Suspect?"

"Nobody's willing to talk with us. We knocked on a few doors, but nobody saw nothing."

Detective Jennings looked at Links before replying.

"I know this kid. He runs with that Black Mob crew. He has a few M.O.B. tattoos on his chest and neck. He's definitely one of theirs. It's going to be some type of retaliation for Links getting smoked."

"We got to get to the bottom of these murders."

Low Life and Scumbag stood in front of STG's corner store chilling, when a black Crown Victoria dipped up on them. Lil Crimey was in the corner store when they rushed. He stashed his bangers and drugs in the chip rack before walking out of the corner store casually.

"Hey, you! Come here!" Detective Jennings yelled.

Lil Crimey walked over to the Detective.

"Is there a problem, Officer," Lil Crimey asked, with a smile on his face?

"Yeah, get your ass up against the wall with your buddies over there," Detective Jennings said, as he pushed Lil Crimey up against the wall aggressively.

Detective Brenton began to check them for drugs and weapons.

"They're clean, partner," Detective Brenton said.

"Which one of you punks killed Links," Detective Jennings asked.

"I don't know nothing about no murders," Lil Crimey replied.

"Word," Low Life added.

"Man, we ain't got nothing to do with no murder. Why y'all fucking with us," Scumbag asked.

"Shut up, asshole. I'm asking the questions around here."

Scumbag sucked his teeth. Detective Jennings pulled out a camera phone and took pictures of Lil Crimey, Low Life, and Scumbag.

"I'm going to be watching all of you little young punks. Until I get to the bottom of these homicides happening in my city, I'm going to be on your ass like white on rice," Detective Jennings said, seriously.

Lil Crimey and his crew remained silent. Detective Brenton was searching the area for drugs but came up with nothing. He un-cuffed them.

"All right, take a walk, all of you! Don't let me catch you on my corners today!" Detective Jennings said.

Lil Crimey and his crew walked back up Barbour Street towards Chappelle Gardens, better known as Holly

65

Wood. Detective Jennings and his partner stood on the corner until Lil Crimey and his crew disappeared into the projects.

As soon as Lil Crimey stepped into the projects, he saw his little cousin, Marlo, spinning tops in the back of the buildings. At the time, Marlo was eight years old going on 20. He emulated everything he saw his cousin, Lil Crimey, and his boys do, and wanted to follow right in his footsteps.

"What up, Blood?" Marlo asked, when he saw his cousin, Lil Crimey.

"What up, Five?" Lil Crimey asked.

"Why the Police had ya'll himmed up?"

"You know we the most hated."

Marlo cracked a smile.

"Let me get some money, Blood."

"I'll give you some money, Five. But I need you to grab my banger and work for me."

"Where it's at?" Marlo inquired.

"In STG's, in the chip rack."

Marlo took off running towards the store before Lil Crimey could say another word. Detective Jennings and his partner, Detective Brenton, were still sitting parked on the corner. Marlo walked past them and went right into the store.

When he got to the chip rack, he began to move the chips to the side. The first thing he noticed was a sandwich bag filled with crack bagged in small 12-12 baggies. He grabbed the drugs and stuffed them in his pants pockets.

As he continued to look through the chips, he saw the butt of a black Glock .40. Marlo grabbed the gun and tucked it in his waistband, like he saw Lil Crimey do on several occasions. Before leaving the store, he grabbed a quarter juice and a bag of Cheese Doodles.

He placed two quarters on the counter. The Puerto Rican man behind the counter looked at Marlo suspiciously, before he walked out of the store. Marlo walked past the Detectives real smoothly. Detective Jennings made eye contact with the young boy, before calling him.

"Hey, kid!" Detective Jennings called out.

Marlo turned around and looked at the Detective.

"Yes, Officer?"

"Why ain't you in school?"

"Half a day," Marlo replied, lying through his teeth, before walking away.

Chapter 17

Daphny laid in her bed in nothing but a t-shirt and panties, with her laptop on her lap, as she sent D-Red an erotic text message.

*　　*　　*

D-Red was laid up in the bed with Unique, when his Nextel alerted him that he had a text message. D-Red slid his body from under Unique's arm, got out of the bed, and snuck off to the bathroom. He began to smile, as he read the text message from Daphny.

The text said, 'I'm laying here all alone in my t-shirt and panties, playing in my box of happiness. Want to join me?'

D-Red began to get aroused, just thinking about planting his face in between her thick thighs. D-Red texted her back.

*　　*　　*

Daphny had two fingers in her love box, as she thought about all the cash D-Red was gone hit her off with. Daphny was a cum freak, and money definitely made her cum. As she pleased herself, the screen on her computer lit up, letting her know she had a text message. Daphny viewed the message.

It said, 'Laid up with wifey. Can't get out tonight.'

Daphny frowned her face up before responding back.

68

Her text message said, 'Too bad. I was finally considering letting you explore every hole.'

*   *   *

When D-Red got the text from Daphny, he wasted no time getting dressed. Unique woke up out of her sleep, when she heard him rambling around in the closet.

"Where you think you're going," Unique asked.

"I gotta make a drop-off."

"At this time of night?"

"Baby, this is business. I got my peoples coming all the way down from VA. I can't keep them waiting on me. They ain't even from around here," D-Red stated.

"So when you coming home?"

D-Red kissed Unique on the lips.

"Don't wait up, baby. I got a couple more drop-offs before I come back home."

Unique sucked her teeth before turning her back to D-Red. D-Red threw on his North Face jacket before leaving their condo. The only thing on his mind was getting to Daphny and all the love she had to give.

*   *   *

Hot 93.7 was bumping in Flava's Beauty Salon on a Saturday afternoon. Women were in the shop in abundance, and the topic of discussion was men. Unique was still thinking about D-Red leaving the house at 2:00 a.m. and not coming home until the next night.

69

They had an argument, and he had left right back out. That had been three days ago. And he hadn't been home since then.

"These niggas out here ain't shit. I done been with Terrence for seven years now, doing his bid with him, sending money, letters, pictures, and all that. Come to find out this nigga got a Facebook page. And guess what his relationship status says," Lauryn said.

"What, girl?" Melony asked.

"Single."

"Huh-uh! Girl, you lying!"

"I'm dead-ass serious," Lauryn stated.

"He need his ass kicked."

"It's all good, though, because I got me a little creep. And Terrence ain't half the man he is."

All the women in the shop started laughing. Unique was never one to put her business in the streets. She knew how shiesty women could be, and knew most of the ladies in the shop would jump at the chance to sleep with her man.

The only person she felt she could confide in was her girl, Melony. After getting her hair done, Melony walked Unique to her car. She could tell something was bothering her, by the troubled look on her face.

"Girl, what's wrong with you?" Melony asked.

"Me and D-Red had an argument about him leaving the house all times of the night."

"Y'all argue all the time. But y'all always patch things up."

"He hasn't been home in three days. I think he's cheating on me," Unique insinuated.

70

Melony hugged her girl, Unique, as tears fell down her face.

"You gone get through this."

*   *   *

D-Red laid back on Daphny's silk sheets, as she rode him like a cowgirl. He gripped her booty, as she jumped up and down on his dick like a porn star. She was working his pole and had him on the verge of exploding. When D-Red couldn't hold back any longer, he began busting off inside the Rough Rider condom he was wearing.

"Ah, shit, baby, I'm cumming!" D-Red yelled.

Daphny slid off him and rolled over onto her back, with a smile on her face. His phone ringing on the dresser took him out of his thoughts.

"Hello," D-Red said.

"Where you at?" Calvin asked.

"Laid up. What's good?"

"I need to holla at you, man."

"Where you at?" D-Red inquired.

"I'm on the block."

"I'll be over there in an hour."

"All right," Calvin stated.

*   *   *

When D-Red finally got to the block three hours later, Calvin was tight. He had no patience for ignorance, and the moves D-Red was making were real sloppy.

"D-Red, what's up, man? I'm getting calls from all our out-of-town clientele telling me you never showed up to handle business," Calvin said.

"That was today? Oh, shit. Ya boy completely forgot."

"That bitch got you all caught up."

"Watch how you talk about Unique," D-Red warned.

"I'm not talking about sis. I'm talking about Daphny. Since you started fucking with her, you been slipping, my nigga."

"I'm good."

"No, you ain't, homey. You gotta tighten up, my nigga. It's a lot at stake right now. This ain't no nickel-and-dime pissy hallway operation. Remember that," Calvin insisted.

"You right," D-Red agreed.

"So when you gone go back home? You got Unique out here stressing like crazy. My sister said she saw her in front of the beauty salon crying her eyes out earlier today."

"Damn!" D-Red said, as he began to think about all the pain he was causing his girl, Unique. "I'm on my way home now. I'm gone need you to handle shit round the way for a couple of days, until I patch things up with Unique."

"I got you."

D-Red gave Calvin dap before jumping in his Range Rover and pulling off.

*   *   *

72

Unique sat in her living room watching *Waiting to Exhale*. Her eyes were puffy from crying all day. And she was hurting emotionally, as thoughts of D-Red in another woman's arms popped into her head. As Angela Bassett burned her husband's car, D-Red walked through the door.

He had a black duffel bag in his hand. Unique looked at him with anger in her eyes, as he advanced towards her. D-Red sat down on the couch next to her. When he saw what movie she was watching, he knew she was heated.

"Bay, we need to talk," D-Red said.

"You damn right we need to talk," Unique replied, as she turned the television off.

"I just want to apologize for being an asshole, ma. You my other half, and when you hurt, I hurt. I never want to hurt you," D-Red said.

"You say you don't want to hurt me. But you always seem to find a way to do just that. Three days, D-Red! It took ya black ass three whole days to find ya way home! What? That bitch you was fucking got tired of you?"

"Come on, bay. It ain't even like that. I would never jeopardize our relationship like that. It's no other woman for me but you, ma. But you gotta understand, baby, that it's gone be some times when I stay out late. But it ain't because I'm trying to do nothing slick. I'm out there getting this money for us, so we can have a better life."

"How long do you think this street shit gone last?"

"Bay, I'm retiring from the game in the next two years," D-Red stated.

73

"How long you been telling me that?"

"Baby, that's my word. You forgive me?"

"You gone work for keeping yo ass out in them streets for three days. What you got in that little black bag of yours? It better be some money, because you definitely taking me shopping," Unique said, as she picked up the duffel bag and unzipped it.

Stacks upon stacks was in the bag. She grabbed a couple stacks out of the bag before putting it back down.

"This should be enough," Unique said, as she scanned through the bills.

D-Red smiled, as he stared into his wifey's sexy eyes.

Chapter 18

Lil Crimey, Low Life, Scumbag, and Tyreik chilled in the project hallway selling crack and drinking Remy.

"Blood, let me get a Dutch," Lil Crimey said.

"I ain't even got none, Five," Tyreik replied.

"I got hella piff with no Dutches," Lil Crimey said, as he pulled out an ounce of piff.

"I'll go grab some," Tyreik volunteered.

"Grab me a grape soda, Blood," Scumbag said.

Tyreik walked out of the building. It was drizzling outside. As he walked to the store, raindrops hit his face. State Property bumped through his MP3 player, as he walked down Barbour Street. Three goons from the other side crept up behind him with guns in-hand.

Their guns began to bust off rapidly. Slugs ripped into Tyreik's back, head, and ass, making him fall to the floor. Prada stood over him and let off two more shots into his back, before they took off running. Lil Crimey jumped up from off the steps, when he heard the gunfire.

"Niggas is busting Blood!" Lil Crimey yelled, as him and his boys ran down the stairs and out the door.

When they got to Barbour Street and saw Tyreik lying lifeless on the pavement, tears filled Lil Crimey's eyes.

"Nah, man! Not my nigga!" Lil Crimey yelled, as he ran over to Tyreik to check for a pulse.

Tyreik was dead. And it was nothing he could do to bring him back. Police sirens could be heard in the distance.

"Come on, Blood. We gotta get low. One Time is coming," Scumbag said, as he grabbed Lil Crimey's arm.

Lil Crimey reluctantly left his boy, Tyreik, and followed his boys back into the building.

* * *

Daphny laid on her bed, on her laptop. She had just sent D-Red a text message letting him know to come through. It was the sixth text message she had sent him that day, and he had yet to hit her back. Daphny wasn't feeling that at all.

She picked up her phone and called his number. But it went straight to voicemail. Daphny closed her computer and laid down thinking about what D-Red was doing that he couldn't call her back. She began to get jealous, as she thought about him spending all his time and money on Unique.

* * *

D-Red carried all of Unique's bags, as she tore the mall up, spending racks of cash at all the high-end fashion stores. Gucci, Fendi, Chanel, and Louis Vuitton were just a few of the brands she was spending all of D-Red's hard-earned money on.

He was still in the doghouse and was doing whatever he had to do to stay in her good graces. He knew Unique was a good girl. And he didn't want to fuck up all the years they had invested in their relationship.

But as much as he loved Unique, he still couldn't get Daphny out of his head. And he knew it wouldn't be long before he was back scratching at her doorstep.

Chapter 19

Political's album *Politics As Usual* had reached number 1 on the Billboard Charts and had sold more than a million copies in the first week. Political and the entire CT Records family celebrated at Mr. Ray Black's new club. Things were looking up for Political and he had no plans of looking back.

*   *   *

A crowd of people stood on Money Martin chilling, when Silk and Ghetto pulled up on a hustler named Leo.

"Leo, come here!" Silk ordered.

'Damn!' Leo thought to his self, as he walked over to the car.

As he got closer, he saw a .50 cal. resting on Silk's lap.

"What's up, Silk, Ghetto?" Leo said, nervously.

"You know what the fuck is up. Where my bread at?" Silk asked.

"I don't got it on me right now," Leo replied.

"Come here! What you got in ya pockets?"

"Come on, Silk. Don't do this to me in front of all these people. Let me grab ya money out of the building."

"Don't play with me, Leo. Bring ya ass right back!" Silk said.

"I got you," Leo replied, before walking into the building.

Silk and Ghetto waited impatiently for Leo to come back. The crowd of people that was in front of the building began to disperse.

"Man, where this nigga at?" Silk asked, as he looked over his shoulder. "Oh, shit! Get down!" Silk yelled, as he pushed Ghetto's head down.

A man dressed in all black with a ski mask ran from the back of the building, busting off an AK-47.

Boc! Boc! Boc! Boc! Boc! Boc! Boc! Boc! Boc! Boc!

Bullets crashed through the doors and windows of Silk's Buick Regal. Silk peeled off with his head low. He got halfway up the block before they crashed into a parked car. Silk and Ghetto jumped out of the car, busting back at the masked man, as they ran through a cut that led to Capen Street. When they got to Capen Street, they hid out in an abandoned building.

"Oh, shit, Silk! You bleeding!" Ghetto said.

"Where?" Silk asked, as he checked his body for gun wounds.

"In your face."

"Them niggas shot me in my face? I'm gone kill them niggas!" Silk said, angrily.

"Oh, nah, that's just a cut from the glass," Ghetto replied, as he pulled the glass out of his boy's face.

"That nigga, Leo, gotta get touched."

"He gone regret the day he ever tried to go against this movement!"

*   *   *

Lil Crimey walked into Leo's gate on Martin Street with his AK-47 in-hand.

"Did you get them?" Leo asked.

"Nah, they got away."

"What? You supposed to kill them! Now they gone be coming for me," Leo said, nervously.

"Man! Sit yo scary ass down. I got everything under control," Lil Crimey replied, before sitting on the La-Z-Boy, putting his feet up on the table, and flipping through the channels until he got to *106 & Park*.

"So when you gone take care of it?"

"You'll be the first one to know, Blood."

Chapter 20

Lisa walked to the phone inside of Danbury Correctional Institution, a women's prison facility. She dialed Jerome's number. She had been trying to call him for the past week, but had yet to get through. Candy was sucking Jerome off something serious when the phone started ringing.

"Hello?" Jerome said.

"You have a collect call from Lisa, an inmate in a State Correctional Facility. To accept, dial five," the automated Operator said.

Jerome sucked his teeth as he pressed five.

"Hello?" Jerome said.

"What's up, baby? I've been trying to call, but I haven't been able to get through," Lisa said.

"I've been out-of-town for a couple of days."

"You like that?" Candy asked Jerome, as she sucked on his dick?

"Who is that?" Lisa asked.

"That was the television, baby. I gotta go," Jerome said, before hanging up on her.

Lisa hung up the phone with a confused look on her face. She walked to her cell. Her celly, Joselyn, was a sexy light-skinned chick who was serving two years for a stolen car that her man was driving her around in. When the Police started chasing him, he got away and she got caught.

The Police tried to make her rat on her boyfriend, but she wouldn't do it. So they gave her two years in a women's prison facility for larceny.

"Lisa, what's wrong? You look sad," Joselyn said.

"I think Jerome is cheating on me," Lisa replied.

"Why you think that?"

"Because when I just called, I heard a woman's voice. But he told me it was the television. He knows that he is wrong for that."

"Do you know who it was?" Joselyn asked.

"Nah."

"It's probably someone close to you that you would least expect."

"Word to my mother. If I find out this nigga cheating on me, it's gone be problems."

* * *

Lil Crimey, Gutta, and a Mob of Bloods stood on the War Zone getting money, when a black Mazda MPV with tinted-out windows rode through the block real slow. Lil Crimey ice grilled the van, as he kept his hand on his .44 Bulldog concealed in his waistband.

"What the fuck that little nigga looking at?" Silk asked, as he drove down Money Martin.

"I'll definitely tighten his little young ass up," Ghetto replied, as he clutched a fully loaded Desert Eagle.

"Look at these little niggas! I know it was one of them clapping at us."

"Pull round the corner. I'm about to get right."

Lil Crimey tapped his man, Gutta.

"Yo, who was that in the MPV van?" Lil Crimey asked.

"I don't know who that was in there, Blood. But them niggas looked real suspect."

82

Lil Crimey walked to the back of the dumpster and grabbed the AK-47, just in case niggas came back through. Lil Crimey had a lot of beef on the street and wasn't trying to get caught slipping.

*   *   *

Mr. Ray Black's eyes rolled to the back of his head, as Shantae sucked him off like a pro. As she did her thing, the only thing running through Mr. Ray Black's head was Melony. She was the perfect girl for him, and he had to have her. When he shot his load, he tossed a couple dollars on the bed and zipped his pants back up.

"Where you going?" Shantae asked.

"I gotta pick up one of my artists from the airport," Mr. Ray Black lied.

Shantae sucked her teeth as she walked to the bathroom to wash her mouth out. Mr. Ray Black didn't care. Since he had met Melony, he had lost interest in Shantae fast.

*   *   *

Silk and Ghetto crept through the cut on Barbour Street that led to the buildings in back of the projects on Money Martin. Lil Crimey heard a twig snap and looked towards the back of the buildings, with the AK-47 pointed that way.

When he saw Silk and Ghetto with guns out, he started clapping at them. They clapped back, as they ran behind the back of the buildings for cover.

83

Boc! Boc! Boc! Boc! Boc! Boc! Boc! Boc! Boc!

"Ah, shit! I'm hit!" Red Rum said, as he fell to the floor.

Lil Crimey continued to let off the AK-47, while Gutta helped Red Rum to the front of the buildings, where his rental was parked. Silk and Ghetto fled the scene, when their ammo got low. Gutta drove Red Rum to the hospital. He had got hit in the foot.

*   *   *

Flava's Beauty Salon was packed on a Friday afternoon. The temperature was up, and so was the gossip.

"Girl, them young boys been acting a fool on Martin Street. Treesha's bad-ass son was out there shooting a gun off that weighed more than his little ass," Donna said.

"What's her son's name?" Melony asked.

"Christopher, but they call him Lil Crimey."

"Ooh, I heard about him. He is bad as hell," Melony replied.

"You know that don't make no sense for them kids to be out there acting a fool like that."

"That's why I'm glad I moved to the suburbs, because ain't nothing but trouble around the way. Anthony is getting older now, and I'll be damned if I have to bury my son."

"I know that's right," Melony replied.

*   *   *

Lisa stood around at mail call while the Correctional Officer called off names for mail.

"Mounds, Rice, Anderson, Jones, Fisher," the Correctional Officer yelled, as he passed out the last of the mail.

"Did you call Kisdale?" Lisa asked.

"Not today, Ms. Kisdale," the Correctional Officer replied, before walking off.

Lisa walked back to her cell mad as hell. She was used to getting mail from Jerome at least three times out the week. But that had slowed down to once every two months, if she was lucky. The only thing he still did for her consistently was send her Money Orders every week.

Her account stayed stacked with cash. But Lisa was in need of love and affection like it used to be between the two of them.

Chapter 21

<u>Melony</u>

Melony grew up in West Brook Housing Projects. As a youth, she spent a lot of time at her grandmother's house.

"Nana, when is my mother coming back?" Melony asked.

"Her and your daddy is taking care of business right now. You gone stay with Nana for a while," Melony's grandmother replied.

Melony cried as her grandmother held her in her arms. She spent many nights like that. But when she came to the realization that the tears wouldn't change a thing, she stopped crying and began to act out in school. She would skip school and hang out with older girls from her project.

They were into everything from smoking weed to selling drugs. When her teachers informed Ms. Watkins about her daughter's behavior, she beat Melony like a runaway slave. But the beatings were only temporary pain.

She would be good for a little while and be right back in the streets. Unique had moved to the projects when Melony was 14. She lived next door to her and was just as bad as her. The girls were introduced by Candy who had been friends with Unique since elementary school.

The girls instantly clicked and began to do everything together, from boosting clothes at the mall to dating boys together. Lewis Fox Middle School days was around the time Melony and Daryl started dating. At the time, he was a pretty-boy cat who had a way with the ladies.

He won Melony over one day, while they were in music class. He passed her a note that explained how he was feeling her. At the bottom of the letter, it was two boxes. And right above it said, if you feeling me, check yes or no.

Melony checked yes and wrote down her phone number. Daryl came to scoop her up in his pop's station wagon that night. Her mother was out with her pops, and she was now old enough to stay in the house by herself. Melony got in the station wagon with him.

Daryl pulled off and parked up in Keney Park. He had a bottle of Jack Daniels that he stole from out his pop's liquor cabinet, and a joint of marijuana. An old-school cut by Brandy was playing on the radio as they got faded.

As the weed and liquor began to take effect, Daryl started kissing Melony. They ended up in the backseat of the station wagon dry-humping for hours. Melony didn't let him hit it that day. But sent him home with sticky boxers and a bad case of blue balls. When she got home, her mother was just getting in.

"Melony, where the hell you been at all night? I been calling and calling, and yo ass ain't pick up the phone," Ms. Watkins said.

"I was next door at Unique's house."

"Did I tell you that you could go over there?"

"No, but I was lonely in this house all day, by myself," Melony lied through her teeth.

"That ain't no excuse not to obey me."

"Annete, leave that girl alone. She wasn't nowhere but next door," Clark said, as he smiled at his daughter.

"You always taking up for her," Annete said, as she walked to the kitchen to fix her a plate of food.

"Because that's my baby girl. Come here, Melony."

Melony ran over to her father and gave him a big hug.

"You iron your clothes for school in the morning?"

"Yes, daddy."

"Here go a couple dollars for lunch money," Clark said, handing her some cash.

"Thanks, daddy."

"You're welcome, sweetheart."

Melony went to her room and began writing in her diary everything that she did that day. After she was done, she put on her pajamas and fell asleep. The next morning, after she took a shower and brushed her teeth, Melony got dressed and walked to school. She saw Unique and Candy standing next to Scott's Jamaican Bakery.

"What up, y'all?" Melony asked.

"Hey, girl. What's going on?" Unique asked.

"Ain't nothing. Me and Daryl hung out yesterday."

"For real? What did y'all do?"

"We kissed and felt each other up. But that's as far as I let it go," Melony informed them.

"What you waiting on?" Unique asked.

"I want to make sure he's the right guy before I just up and give him my virginity."

Daryl walked up a few seconds later.

"What's up, ladies?" Daryl asked.

"Hey, Daryl," Candy and Unique replied in unison.

Daryl kissed Melony on the lips.

"What's up, Bay?" Daryl asked.

"Hi, baby," Melony replied.

"You want to get out of here?"

"I can't skip today. My mother was already bugging me about coming in the house late last night."

"We not gone skip the whole day, just first period," Daryl replied, as he showed her a blunt already rolled up.

"I don't want to ditch my girls."

"They can come, too. Y'all want to hang with ya boy today?"

"I'm down," Unique said.

"Yeah, me, too," Candy added.

Melony reluctantly agreed to hang out with him for a little while. Daryl sparked the blunt and passed a bottle of E&J around that he had stole out his father's liquor cabinet. He drove down Kent Street and saw his boys, Mark and Dolla. They jumped in the backseat with Unique and Candy.

"What up, boy? Pop Dukes let you hold the whip?" Dolla asked.

"He's still hung over from last night. I just grabbed the keys," Daryl replied.

He took a swig from the E&J bottle before passing it to Melony. She took a gulp of the strong brandy, and it burned her chest. She frowned up her face from the strong liquor. Melony passed the bottle to her girl,

Unique, who had no problem downing a nice amount of the liquor.

The weed was circulating, and the liquor had Melony feeling good. Daryl put his hand on her thigh, as he drove around the city. Narcotics Officer Cowboy was driving down Palm Street, when he saw the station wagon full of teenage kids. He busted a bone in the middle of the street and pulled them over.

"Oh, shit. Put that weed out," Daryl said to Melony.

Melony dropped the blunt in between the seats and couldn't find where she dropped it.

"I know I should have went to school," Melony said out loud.

"Just calm down and be cool," Daryl replied, as he sat up in his seat, and tried to look like he was a grown-up.

"How are you doing today, Officer?" Daryl asked, when the Officer came to the window.

"License and registration," Narcotics Officer Billy the Kid ordered.

"I forgot my license at home, Officer," Daryl replied, with a smile on his face.

"Is that marijuana I smell?"

"No, sir."

"Step out of the vehicle," Narcotics Officer Billy the Kid instructed.

Daryl was the first one out of the vehicle and placed in handcuffs.

"Hold this for me," Mark said to Unique, as he tried to pass her a Ziploc bag full of weed.

"Hell no!" Unique replied, as she scooted away from him.

The cop saw the movement in the backseat and pulled everyone out of the car. Once his backup came, a female Officer searched Unique, Candy, and Melony, before placing them in the backseat of a Police cruiser.

"Wait a minute! Why y'all got us back here? We ain't do nothing," Unique said.

"Grand theft auto," Narcotics Officer Billy the Kid said.

"What? We ain't steal no car," Melony barked.

"That's not what Mr. Cummings says."

Daryl's father had called the cops and reported the car stolen. The Police had also found weed on Mark. They were all sent down to the Police Station and allowed to call their parents to come get them. When Melony called her mother and told her what happened, she went ballistic.

As soon as Melony got home, Annete whooped her ass and sent her to her room to think about what she had done. She was also placed on punishment until her mother felt as though she had learned her lesson. The next day, while in school, she bumped into Unique and Candy in the hallway.

"Hey, y'all," Melony said.

"Hey," they replied.

"So what y'all mother say when y'all got home?" Melony asked.

"My sister came and got me, so I got off easy," Candy said.

"My mom was bugging, yo. It's like she act like she never did nothing wrong in her life when she was a kid," Unique said.

"My mother whooped my ass and I'm on punishment."

"Damn! She whooped you and put you on punishment? That's crazy!" Candy replied.

"She don't play."

Daryl walked up to the girls. He had a bruise on the side of his cheek.

"What happened to you?" Melony asked.

"My pops kicked my ass when I got home for stealing his car."

"He punched you?"

"Yeah," Daryl said.

"That's not cool at all," Melony said, as she hugged Daryl.

"I'll be all right. I'm used to it."

"My mother whooped me. But she would never punch me like I'm some stranger on the streets."

"When I get enough cash, I'm out of here," Daryl said.

"Will you take me with you?" Melony asked.

"Definitely."

Melony and Daryl kissed before going to class. By lunchtime, they ended up getting together and sneaking off to a room that had a bunch of computers inside it. They started kissing, as Daryl placed his hands under her dress and squeezed her ass.

She let him slide his hand into her panties and begin to play with her box. Melony wasn't used to that feeling and started moaning out in pleasure.

92

"Lay down."

Melony did as he asked her. Daryl slid her white cotton panties off, spread her thighs, and tried to penetrate her.

"Oh!" Melony moaned, as he got the head inside.

Daryl continued to ease into her, until he had popped her cherry. Daryl began to go faster, as he loved how her virgin walls felt up against his manhood. His face began to twist up when he felt ready to cum. He skeeted off inside of her and pulled out.

He had blood all over his dick, as he looked for something to clean his self off with. Melony gave him a few napkins from out of her bag.

"Thanks," Daryl said, as he wiped his self off.

When they were dressed, they snuck out of the room and went to their classrooms. Melony went home early. She told the nurse that she was having cramps, and they let her leave. When she got home, her mother stopped her at the door.

"Child, what you doing home so early?" Annete asked.

"I been having cramps. The nurse told me to come home early."

"Did I tell you that you could come home early?"

"No, mama," Melony replied.

"That's the problem with you kids now. Just do whatever the hell you want to."

Melony ignored her mother as she walked upstairs and ran herself a hot bath. Her mother looked at her suspiciously when she walked past. Melony soaked her body in the bubble bath and thought about Daryl breaking her virginity.

At first, it was painful for her. But after a while, she started to enjoy it. After her bubble bath, she went to her room to write down everything that happened between her and Daryl. For the next few weeks, Melony and Daryl were creeping around, skipping classes, and having unprotected sex. One day, while Melony was home with her mother, she started throwing up.

"Girl, what's wrong with you?" Annete asked.

"I'm sick," Melony replied, with tears in her eyes.

"You've been throwing up for the last few days. I'm taking you to the hospital."

Melony washed her mouth out before going to the hospital with her mother. She saw Dr. Young. He was her usual Doctor. When Dr. Young informed Melony and her mother that she was pregnant, she couldn't believe it.

"Are you sure, Dr. Young?"

"The tests don't lie, Ms. Watkins. Melony is four weeks' pregnant."

Ms. Watkins looked at her daughter with grief and heartache in her eyes.

"This is what trying to be grown gets you, child. You ain't but 14 and you already having babies. You ain't but a baby yourself."

"I'm sorry, mama."

"Don't be sorry. That's one thing I don't want you to be. You gone have this baby and we gone get through this," Ms. Watkins assured her.

When Melony broke the news to Daryl, he straight stunted on her and acted as if the baby wasn't his. Melony cursed him out and informed him that her and her baby didn't need him. Things were hard for Melony and her child, but they always managed to get by.

Melony ended up getting a job at Flava's Beauty Salon, after school, sweeping up hair. By the time she turned 17, she had her own chair and had graduated from Cosmetology School. Once Daryl realized that Melony and his daughter, Kiara, was doing good without him, he tried to step back into their lives.

But Melony shut him down. Melony felt like he didn't deserve her, and wasn't about to play herself by running back to him.

Chapter 22

Mr. Ray Black sat behind the desk in his office. Moments later, his bodyguard, Damion, walked in.

"Boss, the girl from the other night is here to see you," Damion said.

"Send her in," Mr. Ray Black replied.

Melony strutted into his office dressed in a super tight miniskirt that left little to the imagination. The black leather boots she was wearing gave her a sassy look. Mr. Ray Black couldn't take his eyes off her body, as she walked up to his desk.

"I heard you been asking about me," Melony said, with a seductive smile on her face.

"Yes, Melony. You have been on my mind a lot since we met."

"I'm here now. What are you going to do with me?"

Mr. Ray Black stepped from behind his desk, took Melony into his arms, and began to kiss her passionately. Melony kissed him back, as she slid her small hands into his pants and grabbed his dick. She smiled when she felt how large he was.

"Looks like somebody's happy to see me."

"He has been waiting on you all day."

Melony unzipped his pants and began to stroke his thick, long pipe. Mr. Ray Black bent her over his desk and began to hit it doggy style. Melony's pussy was hot, tight, and wet, just like he imagined. She was throwing it back, while he beat it up. As he began to cum, he yelled out her name.

"Ah, Melony!" Mr. Ray Black yelled.

Shantae smacked Mr. Ray Black on his head. He jumped up out of his sleep mad as hell.

"What you do that for?" Mr. Ray Black asked.

"Who the hell is Melony?" Shantae asked.

"Melony? I don't know anybody named Melony," Mr. Ray Black replied.

"I know when you lying, Ray. You were screaming her name in your sleep!"

Mr. Ray Black sucked his teeth before going to the shower to clean his self off.

"Got my sheets all sticky because you want to be having wet dreams and shit," Shantae replied, as she looked at the wet stains on the sheets.

Mr. Ray Black drowned her voice out, as he let the shower run over his head. He was tired of Shantae and made a promise to cut her off once he got Melony in his life.

*   *   *

Candy and Jerome chilled in Jerome's penthouse, watching *Love Jones*, as they cuddled up on the couch together. Candy had her head resting on his chest, as he held her in his arms. Their relationship began to get more serious, as time went by.

"Baby," Candy said.

"What's up, love?" Jerome asked.

"When you gone tell Lisa about us?"

"Soon, real soon."

"She deserves to know," Candy stated.

"I know."

Melony walked down the aisle in the supermarket looking for low-fat potato chips, when she bumped into Mr. Ray Black.

"Melony, how are you doing?" Mr. Ray Black asked, with a smile on his face.

"Hello, Mr. Ray Black."

"Please, call me Ray."

Melony smiled.

"So, why didn't you call?" Mr. Ray Black asked.

"I don't know. You're not really my type."

"What? Black, handsome, and successful is not your type?"

"I read in the tabloids that you are a player," Melony scoffed.

"You can't believe everything you read in the tabloids. That's not me at all. But the media prints that garbage to sell magazines. It's all business with them. And believe it or not, I prefer to be with one woman. It's too many diseases in the world to be fooling around with more than one woman at a time."

"I agree and strongly believe in a monogamous relationship."

"So can I buy you dinner?" Mr. Ray Black hinted.

"I'm tired of eating out."

"How about I make you dinner?"

"I didn't take you for the cooking type," Melony stated.

"I can definitely work my way around the kitchen."

"I'll give you a call."

"Can I get your number?"

"We will see," Melony replied, before she grabbed her chips and walked off.

Mr. Ray Black watched her ass sway from side-to-side and prayed that she'd call him.

*   *   *

Melony drove home with Mr. Ray Black on her mind. She was feeling him, but didn't want to rush things. When she got home, she jumped in the shower and couldn't get him off her mind. She was hot and bothered. It had been over a year since the last time she had sex with a man.

Her baby father, Daryl, had shitted on her when she got pregnant with Kiara and stopped coming around. He had also denied her baby. Melony was heartbroken because Daryl was the only man she had ever been with. She stressed over him for a while before meeting a hustler named Brick City.

*   *   *

Brick City treated her and her daughter good. He made sure they both had the finer things in life like they deserved. For her 20th birthday, he bought her a brand-new 745i BMW and a bunch of clothes for Kiara. When Melony saw the BMW, she couldn't believe it.

She hugged and kissed him, before driving around the block in it. Melony couldn't have had a better man. Brick City had came down from Newark, New Jersey, and was getting money with his cousin, Demarco, who was from West Brook Housing Projects in Hartford, Connecticut.

They had the work moving throughout the city. Brick City wasn't really the type to deal with too many people. So he let his cousin deal with that end of the business, while he just supplied the work. But no matter how low key you try to be in the game, niggas is gone find out if you getting money or not.

One day, while Melony was in the house playing with her daughter, she got that dreadful call.

"Hello?" Melony said.

"Bay, they got me," Brick City said.

"What? Who got you?"

"We want $100,000, if you ever want to see ya man alive again," the kidnappers said.

"Please don't kill him," Melony cried into the phone.

"You gotta go to my spot and bring that money out the safe," Brick City said, when the kidnappers put him back on the phone.

"I got you, baby," Melony replied, before the phone went dead in her ear.

Brick City had schooled her for situations like these, and gave her the combination to his safe at his crib out in West Hartford. Melony cleaned the safe out when she got to his apartment. She drove back to Hartford and waited for the callers to call. She waited an hour before they called her back.

"You got the money?" the kidnapper asked.

"Yeah," Melony replied.

"Drop it off on Palm Street. You gone see a black Honda Accord sitting parked outside. Open the door and place the money on the seat. Once we count the money and make sure it's all there, we will let your man go."

Melony followed their orders. She sat around and waited for them to call and tell her where to pick up Brick City. But they never called. Brick City was found in an abandoned building with a bullet lodged in his forehead by two crack heads.

His cousin, Demarco, had set him up to get robbed and murdered. He was tired of being the worker and had dreams of becoming a boss.

*   *   *

Brick City's death had Melony in mourning for quite a while. He was the last man she had been with. And now Mr. Ray Black was trying to win her heart. After taking a shower, Melony put on a Carolina Herrera dress with a pair of 3-inch stiletto high heels.

She looked in her full-length mirror and decided to wrap her hair in a bun. When she was dressed, Melony called Mr. Ray Black.

"Hello," Mr. Ray Black said.

"Meet me at the plaza on the Avenue."

"Why can't I just pick you up from your house?" Mr. Ray Black asked.

"Because I don't want you to know where I live," Melony replied.

Mr. Ray Black laughed.

"What do you think I'm going to do? Stalk you?"

"Maybe," Melony replied, with a smile on her face.

"Because I will, only if you want me to."

Melony laughed, also.

"Nah, I'm just playing. I'll be there in five minutes.

*   *   *

Mr. Ray Black was parked in the Plaza on the Avenue when Melony pulled up. He was already in the area, so it didn't take him long to get there. When Melony stepped out of the car, Mr. Ray Black couldn't take his eyes off of her. She looked stunning. He opened the door for her.

"You look beautiful," Mr. Ray Black said.

"Thank you. You look nice, yourself."

"I try," Mr. Ray Black replied, as he admired the thousand-dollar Armani suit he was wearing.

When they got to Mr. Ray Black's crib, Melony couldn't believe how nice the house was.

"This crib is dope!" Melony said, as she looked around the mansion.

"I bought this place from Keith Maretti."

"The videogame designer?"

"Yeah, that's him. He designed that videogame for that famous author from Hartford. What's his name?" Mr. Ray Black asked.

"Richard Warren."

"Yeah, that's him. I like his writing style. He has swag."

"He's my favorite author," Melony stated, smiling.

"I guess I'll have to get you his catalog."

"I already have it."

Mr. Ray Black walked Melony to his private library and took a copy of *The Take Over* from off the shelf.

"You got a copy of this one, too?"

Melony looked at the book and didn't recognize it.

"Where did you get this from? It's not out yet."

"Me and Richard Warren are in the process of doing a soundtrack for his new book, *The Take Over*. So he gave me an exclusive copy before the book was released. He's using a couple of my artists on the soundtrack, so they can get that needed exposure," Mr. Ray Black said.

Melony hugged and kissed him on the cheek.

"Thank you," Melony replied.

"No problem."

Mr. Ray Black walked Melony to the kitchen, where he showed her how he prepared a steak-and-shrimp dinner. Melony was in awe at how good a cook he was. They sat at the kitchen table, while enjoying a candle lit dinner.

The night was perfect, and Melony was feeling the chemistry between them. After dinner, Mr. Ray Black put on some R&B music. They were both tipsy from the champagne they had drunk, while they danced to the music.

Mr. Ray Black stared into her eyes, before they started kissing passionately. Melony kissed him back, as he caressed her breasts and ass.

"I can't do this," Melony said, as she backed away from him.

"Baby, don't fight your heart. You can't win," Mr. Ray Black said, before kissing her again.

Melony pulled back.

"Promise me something."

"What?"

"Promise to never leave me," Melony whispered.

"Baby, I ain't going nowhere," Mr. Ray Black replied, as he held her in his arms and kissed her.

Melony let her guard down and gave in to her heart. They made love by the fireplace, as Darnell Jones played on the sound system.

Chapter 23

Leo pulled up in the parking lot on Money Martin, nervously. He looked from side-to-side, watching his surroundings, as he waited for Lil Crimey. Lil Crimey bopped to the car, dressed in an all-black Army fatigue suit, with a red rag dangling from his back pocket. He had a serious look on his face, as he jumped into Leo's car.

"What up, Blood?" Lil Crimey asked.

"You tell me. Did you get them yet?" Leo asked.

"Nah, not yet. But them niggas gotta get it. They shot my homey, Red Rum, the other night."

"You gotta take care of this, Lil Crimey. I'm out here looking over my shoulder, left and right."

"I got it under control. You got something for me?"

Leo dug in his pocket and gave Lil Crimey a wad of cash.

"Me and the team going out to the club tonight. Let me hold the Cartier specks," Lil Crimey said.

Leo took off his $2,500 designer frames and passed them to Lil Crimey. He knew it would be the last time he would see the glasses again. But it was a small price to pay to get Silk and Ghetto off his neck.

*   *   *

Silk sat parked on Bed Roc eating a dish of stew fish, dumplings, and rice, and peas, when a dope fiend named Grease Ball walked up to his rental. Silk rolled down the window.

"What up, Grease Ball?" Silk asked.

"It's some kids around the corner that look like they about to bring you a move, neph. I heard one of them mention ya name," Grease Ball said.

Silk threw Grease Ball a bundle of dope.

"Good looking, Grease Ball," Silk said, as he threw the plate of food in the driveway and jumped out of his rental.

As he walked across the street, Lil Crimey and Gutta came around the corner busting at him.

Boc! Boc! Boc! Boc! Boc!

Silk dumped back, as he ran towards the building. Lil Crimey closed one eyelid and aimed at Silk as he ran.

Boc! Boc! Boc!

Two slugs hit Silk in the shoulder, and one hit him in the back. He fell to the ground face-first, right before he got to the side of his building. Lil Crimey and Gutta walked towards the side of the building to finish the job. But when they got there, Silk was gone.

A trail of blood was on the grass that led to the backyard. As they followed the trail, sirens could be heard in the distance.

"Come on, Blood! We gotta get out of here," Gutta said.

"Damn!" Lil Crimey replied, as he reluctantly followed his boy.

Silk was breathing heavy with his gun in his hand, as he stood in the back hallway, waiting for his attackers to enter. His baby mother called his phone, when she heard the shots and saw his rental parked outside. His phone was on vibrate, so it didn't make any noise.

"Hello," Silk said.

"Baby, where you at?" Denise asked.

"Open the backdoor," Silk replied.

When Silk got in the house, Denise went hysterical from the sight of all the blood. Ghetto came out the backroom with Simone on his heels. He went ballistic when he saw his boy hit up.

"I gotta get you to a hospital! What happened?" Ghetto asked, as he helped his boy outside to his rental.

"Them little niggas from the War Zone caught me slipping."

"I'm gone murder them niggas!" Ghetto replied, as he rushed his boy to the hospital on Woodland Street.

He stashed the hammers under the seat, before helping him inside of the hospital.

"I need a Doctor! My boy has been shot!"

The paramedics rushed Silk inside of the Emergency Room. Ghetto hoped and prayed that his boy made it. He was definitely ready to turn the beef up a few notches.

*   *   *

Ghetto walked down the War Zone with his fitted hat low and his head down. Manny and Nice were on the block selling weed and drinking Seagram's Gin in front of the buildings, when Ghetto pulled out a .44 Bulldog and started busting at them.

The first shots hit Manny in the neck and face. Nice tried to run, but Ghetto shot him in the back. Nice fell to the ground. Ghetto was advancing towards him, when a hail of bullets came his way, barely missing his head.

Boc! Boc! Boc! Boc! Boc!

Lil Crimey ran out the building, busting a chrome-and-black .45 at Ghetto. Ghetto backpedaled up the block busting back, before running in between the buildings that led to Nelson Street. When he got to Nelson Street, he jumped in his rental and peeled off.

Chapter 24

Melony, Unique, and Candy walked around the Buckland Hills Mall with bags of designer clothes and shoes in-hand.

"Let's go to the food court," Unique suggested.

The ladies walked into the food court and ordered food from Burger King. As they sat at their table, a dusty-looking kid walked over to the ladies' table with a bop in his step.

"What's up, ma? Can I holla at you for a second?" the boy asked, looking at Unique.

Unique looked the boy up and down, starting with his dirty fitted hat, all the way down to his busted Nike Uptowns. She frowned her face up.

"Not! What you need to do is get ya little dusty ass up out my face, while I'm eating," Unique replied, before snaking her neck and rolling her eyes.

The boy looked to the ground, as he walked back to his table, embarrassed. Candy put her hand over her mouth in shock of how her girl had just dissed the boy.

"Unique, you ain't have to go that hard on him," Candy said.

"Nah, he asked for that one, coming over here looking like he just got finished playing in the sandbox. If you don't get ya dusty ass out of here, he ain't even have a haircut, ill," Unique said, as she frowned her face up.

Melony and Candy couldn't help but laugh at her dramatics. After the ladies were done eating, they walked towards the Gucci store. Melony looked across the mall and saw Richard Warren signing autographs in Barnes and Noble.

"Oh my God!" Melony said.

"What, girl?" Unique asked, curiously.

"There go my boo!"

"Who?"

"Richard Warren, he over there in Barnes and Noble signing books. Let's go take a picture."

The girls walked into Barnes and Noble. Richard Warren was behind a table signing autographs. Melony walked over to the author and gave him a hug.

"Richard, what's up? Why didn't you tell me you would be in town?" Melony asked.

"I just got back today from a world-wide tour. I'm promoting my new book, *The Take Over*."

"I have to get a picture with you, before you go."

"We can do that."

Richard Warren signed their copies of his newest book, *The Take Over*, and took a few pictures with the ladies, before Melony and her girls left the mall.

*   *   *

Lil Crimey walked down Money Martin with a hood over his head. A light drizzle of rain came down, as he walked up the block. He put on a mean mug when he saw Melvin, a kid from the Avenue, jump out a black Mazda MX6 turbo and run to the truck.

Lil Crimey stood on the side of the corner store on Martin Street side, with his .45 in-hand. A few minutes later, Melvin was walking back to his car when Lil Crimey pulled his heat out on him.

110

"Run everything, Blood!" Lil Crimey said, as he put his gun to the kid's head.

"Come on, Great. Don't do it like that. I don't even be with the bullshit," Melvin said.

Lil Crimey smacked him in the back of the head with the gun.

"Shut up!" Lil Crimey said, as he dug in the boy's pockets and took his money, phone, and drugs. "Take them motherfucking jewels off, too, Blood."

Melvin took off his chain, rings, and bracelet.

"Let me get them bottles and that AVIREX, too."

"Damn, Kik, you gone even take my AVI?"

Lil Crimey cocked back the .45, not bothering to respond. Melvin took the jacket off and gave it to Lil Crimey along with the bottles.

"Get the fuck out of here, Blood! You know you should be dead right now. But I'm gone give ya bitch ass a pass! Don't let me see you in my hood no more!"

The kid jumped back in his whip and peeled off. The only reason he wasn't dead right now was because him and Lil Crimey had grew up together, and went to the same school, all the way up to high school. Melvin is originally from the War Zone.

But his family moved to the Avenue three years ago. Melvin started hanging with niggas from the Deuce. When Lil Crimey heard about that, he banned Melvin from the hood. Lil Crimey walked back down the block to the projects on Money Martin.

It had stopped raining, and a few chicks and some dudes were outside. Lil Crimey and Gutta chilled in front of the buildings and drunk the bottles of Remy Martin that Lil Crimey had just took from Melvin. When

111

they were down to the last bottle, two black Mazda MX6 turbos came speeding up the block.

The Ave Boys hung out the window clapping at Lil Crimey and the crowd of people that were on the block. A bullet hit Kenny in the leg and a girl named Rosalyn in the stomach. Lil Crimey blasted at the Ave Boys, as they sped away. Kenny and Rosalyn were rushed to the hospital by ambulance.

*   *   *

South Boy, a well-known get money nigga from Lenox Street, walked down his back steps with a duffel bag full of cash and drugs. His cell phone was ringing off the hook with weight sales. When he got to the bottom flight of stairs, Lil Crimey stepped from the side of the building with a sawed off 12-gauge Mossberg pump in his hand.

"You know what it is, Blood! Run everything!" Lil Crimey ordered.

South Boy knew the young boy had a rep on the streets for slumping niggas. So he didn't play no games with him. He tossed the duffel bag to Lil Crimey.

"Take them jewels and Cartiers off, too, Fam!"

South Boy took his jewels and glasses off. He passed them to Lil Crimey.

"Now, I gotta put you in the ground with ya niggas!" Lil Crimey said.

Block walked to the backyard to grab his pack and saw his boy, South Boy, getting robbed. He pulled out a .380 and started busting at Lil Crimey. Lil Crimey banged back with the pump, making Block run behind the building for cover.

Lil Crimey ran through the cut that led to the next block over. He could hear bullets whizzing past his head, as he barely escaped death. When he got to his whip and jumped in the passenger's seat, his baby mother peeled off. The Ave boys blasted at the whip. Lil Crimey banged back, as they made a smooth getaway.

*   *   *

Snow hung on the War Zone with his baby mother, Rasheeda. She was looking right in the Grown & Sexy shorts set that clung to her body just right.

"So what we gone do tonight? We at your spot?" Snow asked.

Rasheeda smiled.

"What time you coming over?" Rasheeda asked.

Before Snow could respond, a black Nissan Maxima pulled up and the occupants of the vehicle started blasting. Snow hid behind his baby mother, as bullets riddled her body. The Nissan Maxima peeled off. Snow cried, as he held his baby mother in his arms. When the Detectives arrived on the scene, they questioned Snow.

"Son, who did this?" Crooked Chris asked.

"I don't know," Snow replied.

"Come on, son. You have to work with us if you want the men responsible for this murder put behind bars."

"I said I don't know! They were wearing masks."

"We're going to need a statement from you."

After the Police were done interrogating him, Snow went back to his hood. Lil Crimey was in front of his house, ready for war.

"I heard what happened to Rasheeda. We gone body all them niggas, Blood!" Lil Crimey said.

"Nah, man, I can't do it," Snow replied.

"What?"

"I'm gone leave it in God's hands. He will take care of it."

Lil Crimey sucked his teeth, before walking away from Snow.

Chapter 25

D-Red drove down Murda Field with the music bumping. He had *The Best of Queens Bridge Part 2* bumping, when he pulled up on Militant One. Militant One jumped in the passenger's seat.

"What up, Kik?" D-Red asked.

"Let me get a box of dope," Militant One replied, before handing D-Red a wad of cash.

D-Red passed Militant One the dope.

"Yo, be safe out here. You know the Narcs been out here. It's TNT day," D-Red said.

"Nah, they better be safe while I'm out here. These are my streets," Militant One said, before lifting his shirt and showing D-Red the C4 that was strapped around his stomach.

D-Red looked on in shock, as Militant One hopped out of the car. He knew the kid wasn't all there, and wouldn't hesitate to go all out if he was pushed.

*   *   *

Leo and Jernae walked into a soul food spot on Main Street called Mama Jenkins' Soul Food. They were dressed nicely. Jernae had on a strapless dress made by Dolce and Gabana, and Leo was wearing a designer business suit made by Calvin Klein.

He had just met Jernae and wanted to impress her. So he brought her to church, and now they were eating at a soul food spot. They had met at the Sportsmen. Leo had paid for all of the Bloods from the War Zone to get up in the club.

His reason for doing this was for security purposes only. He knew, as long as he was surrounded by them, nobody would try to get at him. Jernae had walked past them, looking right in a Grown & Sexy cat suit that looked painted on.

Her ass bounced from side-to-side, as she walked past. Leo didn't waste any time sending a bottle of Ciroc over to her table. She smiled in Leo's direction. He walked over to her table and introduced his self. After they were properly introduced, they hung out for the rest of the night, drinking and smoking lamb spread.

After the club, Leo asked her to come up to his place for a nightcap. But she declined. They exchanged numbers and promised to get together the next day.

"So, do you see anything you like?" Leo asked.

"Is that a trick question?" Jernae asked.

"Only if you want it to be," Leo replied, with a smile on his face.

"Boy, you're so fresh. Let me think. The fried fish dinner sounds good."

Their waiter came to their table.

"How may I help you guys today?" the waiter asked.

:Let me get the fried chicken, and she'll have the fried fish dinner," Leo said.

"And for dessert?"

"Apple pie."

"And I'll have the pecan pie.

"What type of drinks?" the waiter continued.

"Sprite and Pepsi."

The waiter came back with their drinks before the food arrived. When their order arrived, Leo wasted no time digging into his meal.

"Baby, wait, you have to say grace. Bow your head," Jernae said.

Leo did as she said. Jernae dropped cyanide into his drink. After grace was said, Leo dug into his food. He took a sip of his drink to wash down the food.

"This is good," Leo said, in between bites.

Seconds later, he grabbed for his heart. The poison had taken effect and killed him instantly. Jernae got up from her seat and walked out of the restaurant, as a crowd of people gathered around Leo. She jumped in the passenger's seat of Ghetto's rental.

"It's done," Jernae said.

Ghetto smiled, before pulling off in the black-on-black Chevy Impala.

*   *   *

Detective Jennings and Detective Brenton walked into Mama Jenkins' Soul Food. Leo was laid out on the floor, dead as a door knob.

"What we got here?" Detective Jennings asked.

"Witnesses say he was out dining with an attractive African-American woman in her early 20s, when all of a sudden he just fell out and died," a young Detective stated.

"Where's the woman he was with?"

"Witnesses say she walked out, as soon as the body dropped."

117

"Do you think she had something to do with his demise?" Detective Jennings pressed on.

"The way it's looking, she definitely had something to do with it. Once an autopsy is done, we will be able to determine exactly what the cause of death was."

"Who owns this place?"

"A woman named Tina Jenkins. She's in the back," the young Detective informed him.

The Detectives walked to the back of the restaurant where Mama Jenkins was at.

"Ms. Jenkins," Detective Brenton said.

"Yes? That's me," Mama Jenkins replied.

"I'm Detective Brenton and this is my partner, Detective Jennings. We need to ask you a few questions."

"Okay."

"Where were you when Leo Crews died?" Detective Brenton inquired.

"In the back, cooking. Today was a busy day, so I didn't leave the back at all."

"Who served Leo and the woman he was with?"

"My nephew, Steven," Mama Jenkins stated.

"We need to speak with him."

"Steven!" Mama Jenkins called out.

Steven walked into the back.

"These Detectives need to speak with you."

"Steven, do you remember how the woman looked who was with the man who died?"

"We keep surveillance tapes," Mama Jenkins cut in.

"Do you mind showing us?" Detective Brenton asked.

Mama Jenkins walked into her office and played back the surveillance tape.

"We're going to need this tape," Detective Brenton said, before grabbing the tape.

He had noticed Jernae place something into Leo's drink, but couldn't tell exactly what it was. When they got down to the Police Station and scanned through mug shots on the computer, they saw a mug shot of the girl from Mama Jenkins' Soul Food Spot.

Her real name was Jernae Edwards. She had been arrested for check fraud in the past, but had just graduated to murder.

*   *   *

Ghetto had got a call from his cousin, Jernae. She was mad nervous and going hysterical, as she spoke to him.

"Ghetto, what I'm gone do? They got a Warrant out for me for murder! They been showing my picture on the news all day!"

"Jernae, calm down! Where you at?"

"I'm still at the spot you got for me," Jernae indicated.

"I'm on my way. Don't go anywhere."

"All right."

Ghetto hung up the phone.

"Who was that?" Silk asked.

He had just got out of the hospital and was still recovering from his gun wounds.

119

"That was my cousin, Jernae. She sounds like she's ready to crack," Ghetto replied.

"You know what you gotta do."

Ghetto looked at his boy seriously but didn't reply.

*　　　*　　　*

Jernae was in the apartment Ghetto had got for her packing up her clothes, when Ghetto walked in. She hugged him tightly, as tears rolled down her eyes.

"Cuz, I don't know what I'm gone do! They got me on the news like I'm some type of terrorist or something," Jernae said.

"Did you tell anybody about you poisoning Leo?"

"No, I didn't tell anybody."

"How did they find out?" Ghetto asked.

"The surveillance footage from the restaurant."

"I'm gone take care of all your problems," Ghetto replied, as Jernae packed up all her bags.

"I'm gone need some cash," Jernae replied.

"You ain't gone need no cash where you going, baby girl."

"What?" Jernae asked, as she looked up at Ghetto.

Ghetto had tears in his eyes, as he pulled the trigger, shooting his favorite cousin three times in the chest and face. Jernae died with her eyes open. Ghetto closed her eyes, as tears rolled down his face.

*　　　*　　　*

Lil Crimey walked up the War Zone with Real Deal.

120

"Somebody poisoned the homey, Leo," Gutta said.

"That shit been on the news all day, Blood. The bitch he was with got slumped at her apartment," Lil Crimey replied.

"That whole situation is mad suspect."

"Word to Blood."

Chapter 26

<u>D-Red</u>

D-Red grew up on Belden Street. As a youth, he was introduced to the game at an early age, by a Puerto Rican cat named Carlos, who was dating his sister. D-Red started out pumping bundles of dope for Carlos, but quickly worked his way up to ounces of raw.

He was a little nigga getting his cake up and pushing a crisp Honda Accord, with chrome rims and a booming system. He always knew Unique since they were kids. But she never showed any interest in him until he started getting money.

"Unique, what's up? Can I holla at you for a minute?" D-Red asked.

"This ya ride?" Unique asked, as she walked over to his car.

"Yeah, this me. I'm trying to take you to go see that new movie *Crush Groove*. You with it?"

Unique thought for a minute, already knowing what she was going to say.

"Call me," Unique replied, before writing her phone number on the palm of his hand.

He pulled off, bumping a track from Run DMC. Unique was feeling everything about D-Red. His swag, style, and aura had her wide open off of him. When she went to her house, she called her best friend, Candy, so she could loan her an outfit for her date with D-Red. Candy always kept some fly shit to wear in her closet.

"Hello," Candy said.

"Hey, girl. What you doing?"

"Nothing, just watching my stories."

"Guess who asked me out today," Unique said, anxious.

"Who?"

"D-Red's fine ass."

"Dope-selling D-Red?" Candy inquired.

"Yeah."

"Girl, you better be careful. These girls is out here chasing after that boy left and right."

"You know when he get a taste of all this chocolate, he ain't gone want no other flavor," Unique bragged.

"I know that's right. So where y'all going?"

"He taking me to the movies to see *Crush Groove*."

"I heard that movie is dope. I ain't get to see it yet," Candy said, disappointed.

"You want me to see if he got a friend?"

"Nah, I supposed to be going to see it with Rondell this weekend."

"That reminds me. You got something I can wear tonight?" Unique inquired.

"Girl, you know I got you. Come over."

Unique walked next door to Candy's apartment and picked out a cute little skirt set that revealed a lot of skin and cleavage. When D-Red picked Unique up, he couldn't take his eyes off of her. She looked good, and his hormones was fucking with him.

"You look nice," D-Red said, as he admired her thick and chocolate thighs.

"Thank you," Unique replied.

Every time Unique turned her head, she noticed

D-Red checking her out. When he pulled up at the movie theater and bought tickets, popcorn, and Goobers for them, they went to the back of the theater and started making out. D-Red was all over her. When he tried to slide his hand in between her thighs, she wouldn't let him.

"Stop, baby! Let's watch the movie," Unique said.

D-Red chilled out for about two minutes before he was all over her again. They kissed, and she let him feel a little thigh and ass. But that was as far as she went with him that night. They went on a few more dates before D-Red got the skins in the backseat of his Honda Accord, in Keney Park.

He couldn't believe his luck. Unique was a virgin. His first intentions was just to fuck her and keep it moving. But when they had sex, he was open and couldn't see his self without having her in his life. D-Red moved Unique in with him, but made sure she stayed in school and got her education.

They had their own apartment on the south end. D-Red laced her with all the designer clothes that the big-time hustlers were buying their girls. He also copped her a Toyota Camry and jewelry on a regular basis. Unique and D-Red was living comfortably until one day niggas broke into their apartment and got them for mad cash, drugs, jewelry, and clothes.

D-Red didn't see that shit coming and was down to about 20 bundles of heroin to his name. He had been down before and told his self he would get back on his feet in no time. D-Red took it back to the block and was grinding hard.

He was on the block from early morning all the way until late night, trying to recoup that bread. He was standing on Belden Street early morning, when a green pickup truck pulled up on the block. He and two other cats rushed the sale.

"Yo, what up? I got that fire," a young hustler said.

"Let me get a bundle," the white boy said.

As soon as the young hustler served the fiend, the blue Taurus dipped around the corner. A couple of hustlers tossed packs on the ground, as they ran up the block. More Narcs ran from the back of the buildings with guns drawn.

"Freeze! Up against the wall!" Narcotics Officer Crooked Chris yelled.

"Damn!" D-Red said, as he was placed in handcuffs and put in a patty wagon, along with the rest of the hustlers who were out there.

*   *   *

As D-Red sat in the holding cell, he saw a kid from his neighborhood named Ghetto. He was an older hoodlum who stayed locked up.

"Yo, D-Red. What up, baby? What you got bagged for?" Ghetto asked.

"The Narcs rushed the block and found somebody else pack."

"Damn, that's tough. Niggas ain't claim they shit?"

"Man, hell, nah. I still got my pack on me," D-Red informed him.

"Word?"

"Yeah. I got a couple bundles on me."

"Yo, I know you don't want to get bagged trying to sneak that shit in the Meadows. Let me get it through for you. I know all them COs up in here. They will let me rock."

D-Red slid the bundles of dope across the hall, wrapped up in a brown paper bag that the bagged lunches had come in. Ghetto grabbed the drugs and tucked them in between his ass cheeks.

"Yo, I'll see you tomorrow, Ghetto. I'm about to lay it down. I'm tired as hell."

"All right, little homey."

The next morning, when D-Red went in front of the Judge, his bond was raised and he was sent to the Meadows. After being strip-searched, D-Red was placed in a holding cell until he saw Medical. When he was called to Medical, D-Red spotted his boy, Calvin, sitting on a bench.

"Calvin, when you got up in here?" D-Red asked.

"They came through Center Street and snatched me up last night," Calvin replied.

"What you got bagged with?"

"The .40 cal."

"Damn, what they talking about?" D-Red inquired.

"The Judge called me a menace to society and raised my bond."

"Judge Bloomenthal on some bullshit! He raised mine's, too."

D-Red saw Ghetto walk out of the bathroom.

"Yo, Ghetto, what up? You got that for me?" D-Red asked.

"I ain't got shit for you, little nigga!" Ghetto replied, changing his whole attitude and demeanor.

126

"Word? It's like that?"

"Yeah, it's like that! What's up?" Ghetto asked.

Calvin jumped up off the bench.

"D-Red, what's up? This nigga owe you something?" Calvin asked.

"What the fuck you gone do, little nigga? I'll tighten ya little ass up, too," Ghetto said.

"Nigga, suck my dick! You ain't gone do shit to me, bra!" Calvin replied, as he mean mugged Ghetto.

Ghetto began to advance toward Calvin, when Correctional Officer Weaver stepped from out of Medical.

"Is there a problem?" Correctional Officer Weaver asked.

"Nah, there's no problem, Officer," Ghetto replied, with a smile on his face.

"You two, come with me. Rickers, I don't want any trouble out of you. I'll have your ass in Segregation so fast you won't know what hit you," Correctional Officer Weaver warned Ghetto.

Ghetto ignored the Correctional Officer. Correctional Officer Weaver knew what Ghetto was about, and had witnessed him stab a Solidos gang member back in 1988, when that gang shit was really popping in the hood.

"Man, you can't be letting niggas try to play you, bra. If you let a nigga get away with it once, he gone keep trying to play you," Calvin said to D-Red.

"Fuck that nigga! Let him have that shit!" D-Red replied.

Calvin shook his head, because D-Red wasn't understanding what he was trying to tell him. When

127

D-Red got to his housing unit, he called up Unique. She answered on the second ring.

"Hello?" Unique said.

"You have a collect call from D-Red, an inmate in a state correctional facility. To accept the call, press five."

Unique accepted the call before the Operator could finish.

"Hey, baby," Unique said.

"What's up, love?"

"I spoke with your Lawyer today. And he said he's going to need some more money for your case."

D-Red sucked his teeth.

"You gotta go see Carlos. You remember the spot, right?"

"Yeah, I remember."

"He will take care of my Lawyer fees," D-Red said.

"All right."

"So what's been going on?"

"I miss you, baby," Unique whined.

"I miss you, too, and you know we gone get through this. I just need you by my side right now."

"I ain't going nowhere, baby."

"Make sure you write and send me pictures. You know that's what a nigga need up in here," D-Red stated.

"I sent you $50 so you can get you some commissary, too."

"Good looking, I'll call you tomorrow, baby."

"Bye, I love you," Unique assured him.

"I love you, too."

When D-Red hung up the phone, he went back to his cell and laid down. He was stressed out and going through it already.

Chapter 27

Unique sat in the apartment D-Red had got her on the south end, with Melony and Candy. His cell phone was ringing off the hook.

"Damn! That phone don't stop ringing, do it?" Candy asked, as she took a pull off a blunt of skunk weed.

"Them is D-Red's customers. They don't know he's locked up," Unique replied.

"So what you gone do? You gotta pay the rent on this apartment. You still got Lawyer fees for D-Red. And you have to live," Candy said.

"I don't know what I'm gone do, y'all," Unique replied, with a worried look on her face.

*   *   *

The next day, Unique went to Carlos' bodega on Franklin Avenue. A small girl was at the cash register when she walked in.

"I'm here to see Carlos," Unique said.

"Carlos!" the girl yelled out.

Carlos walked from the back of the store. He was an overweight man who dressed in Italian suits and designer shoes.

"What can I do for you?" Carlos asked.

"I need to discuss some business with you," Unique replied.

Carlos walked to the back of the store. Unique followed him. As soon as she stepped into the backroom, he pulled her to him, covered her mouth, and began to search her to see if she was wearing a wire.

The only thing running through Unique's mind was, 'Please don't let him rape me.'

Carlos let her go when he didn't find the wire.

"What was all that about?" Unique asked.

"Me and D-Red have done business for quite some time now. But in this business, your own family will cross you to save their own ass. You can never be too careful. But now that we got that out of the way, what can I do for you?"

"I need some product," Unique replied.

"Some product?" Carlos asked, with a smile on his face.

"Yeah, I gotta pay my man's Lawyer fees and our bills."

Carlos looked at her with lust in his eyes.

"A girl as beautiful as you shouldn't have to deal with all those problems. I know if you were my woman, you'd be well-taken care of," Carlos said.

"I'm a big girl and was raised to take care of myself," Unique said, as she handed him $1500.

It was all the cash she had in the world. Carlos looked at the cash like it was poisonous.

"What?" Unique asked.

"Do you think I deal with nickel-and-dime hustlers? If I choose to deal with you, it will be in heavy weight. Do you think you can move a kilo of heroin?"

"I know I can," Unique replied.

Carlos pulled a kilo of heroin from out of a black duffel bag.

"Bring me back $90,000."

Unique put the kilo of heroin into her Coach bag and left the store. As she drove back to her apartment, she was nervous as hell. Unique knew if the Police would have pulled her over, and found the drugs, they would most definitely try to bury her. When Unique got inside of her apartment, she felt a little more safer.

D-Red had taught her how to bag and cut up dope, when he was home. So she knew exactly what she had to do. Unique bagged up 100 bundles of dope before hitting the block and serving the fiends off her phone. A young boy no older than 15 named Loco sat back and watched, as she hustled out in the open.

He shook his head, because he knew she was like a baby lamb swimming in shark-infested waters. He had a cigarette in his hand, as she got money.

"Shorty, let me holla at you for a second," Loco said.

Unique looked at the young boy, wondering what he wanted.

"What's up?" Unique asked.

"You know what you doing out here is a total violation, right?" Loco asked.

"What you talking about?"

"How you gone try to hustle over here, and you ain't even from over here? I understand ya man moved you in the building. But that don't give you the green light to step on nobody else's toes. You see that kid over there across the street with the black hood on?"

"Yeah," Unique replied.

"That nigga's ready to lay you down. You out here slipping and not being aware of your surroundings."

Unique stepped into the hallway. The kid across the street dressed in all black crept back into the darkness. Unique started crying.

"What I'm supposed to do? I got bills that need to be paid, and I got to make sure my boyfriend's Lawyer's paid off."

"How much you sitting on?"

"I got a little something. Why?" Unique asked, not really trusting Loco.

"You said you needed some help, right? I got you."

"How you got me?"

"I'm gone help you move it," Loco indicated.

Unique had about 65 bundles on her. She gave them to Loco.

"How do I know I can trust you?"

"Because if I wanted to burn you, Shorty, you would be hog-tied in your apartment right now with a bullet lodged in ya forehead," Loco said, seriously.

"So how do I get in contact with you?"

"You don't. I'll call you."

Unique went back upstairs. She had made enough money to pay D-Red's Lawyer off and pay her bills for a little while. The phone continued to constantly ring, but she decided not to bring anymore of D-Red's clients to the south end.

She had them meet her in West Brook. After not hearing from Loco in two days, she just knew he had burned her. She had copped a .38 revolver and planned on putting a hot one in him, whenever she saw his little ass.

A knock at her front door took her out of her thoughts. She opened the door and saw Loco standing there with a smile on his face.

"Boy, where the hell you been?" Unique asked.

"I was handling my business," Loco replied, as he dropped three knots of money on her kitchen table. "You thought I was gone burn you, didn't you?"

"I thought I was gone have to come looking for you with my pistol."

"Girl, stop playing. You know that's what I do," Loco replied, as he showed her a black 9 Beretta.

"So what's next?" Unique asked.

"The fiends is going crazy for this shit. Where did you get this?"

"From a friend," Unique replied, not wanting to reveal too much information.

"Well, you need to get some more of that."

"I already have."

Unique walked to the backroom and came back out with 200 bundles of dope. She passed the work to Loco.

"I'll holla at you when I'm done," Loco said.

"All right."

Unique was running through the dope at a fast pace. The fiends on D-Red's phone couldn't get enough of it, and Loco had the south end on lock. It didn't take Unique long to pay Carlos his $90,000.

"Unique, I'm impressed. I didn't think you would be able to pull it off so fast," Carlos said.

"I don't play when it comes to getting money," Unique replied.

"I like that."

Carlos gave Unique 3 kilos of heroin.

"Come see me when you're done," Carlos said.

"I will," Unique replied, before leaving.

Chapter 28

Loco stood on the block gambling, when Cito, the kid who was gone rob Unique, ran from in back of the building dressed in all black with a .357 revolver in his hand. Loco pulled out his 9 Beretta and let Cito have it. He shot the stickup kid in the face, chest, and shoulder in front of everybody.

Cito began to twitch uncontrollably, as he took his last breath. The crowd of people that were outside ran in all different directions. Loco walked away casually. Murder was nothing new to him. Unique heard the shots from her window, and ducked down to the floor. She was no fool. And sure wasn't trying to get hit by a stray bullet.

*   *   *

The next day, Unique was up early. She had plans to flood the block with work. When she heard someone picking the lock, she grabbed for her gun that was on the table. She pointed the gun at D-Red, as he walked into the apartment. He jumped back when he saw her pointing the gun at him.

"Unique, what the hell are you doing?" D-Red asked.

Unique dropped the gun on the couch, ran over to her man, and gave him a big hug.

"Baby, you're home! How you get out?" Unique asked.

"They gave me probation," D-Red said, as he looked around the apartment.

He noticed drug paraphernalia and the 3 kilos of heroin Unique had gotten from Carlos, on the table.

"Unique, what the hell is this?" D-Red asked.

"Ya baby was holding it down while you was gone. I went to see ya connect like you said, and he fronted me some work."

"Unique, I never told you to get no work from him! All I told you to do was go get some money from him for my Lawyer. That was it. What if you had gotten busted? Then what would we have done?"

"I'm sorry, baby. I should have told you. But I just did what I felt was right for us," Unique stated.

"Where was you hustling at?"

"Ya boy, Loco, helped me sell most of the work."

"Loco?" D-Red said, surprised.

"Yeah."

"Unique, stay away from him. That boy is dangerous."

"Loco is all right," Unique replied.

"Unique, listen to what I'm telling you. You don't know him like I do."

"Okay."

"Where's the money you made?" D-Red inquired.

Unique went into the room and came back out with a sneaker-box full of cash. D-Red put the cash in a book bag before leaving.

"Baby, where you going?" Unique asked.

"To pay back the connect for the work he fronted you."

When D-Red got to Carlos' store, he was in the back smoking a Cuban cigar and drinking Bacardi rum. He smiled, when he saw D-Red.

136

"D-Red, what's up, Papi?" Carlos asked.

"Hey, Carlos."

"Welcome home. A friend of mine told me you got probation."

"Yeah, they knew they really didn't have a strong case, so they had no choice but to give me probation. How you going to charge eight people with the same package?" D-Red informed him.

"The judicial system plays a lot of games."

"That, they do."

"Have a drink with me," Carlos suggested.

"I have to go see my Probation Officer. I just wanted to drop this off to you."

"What's this?"

"About $90,000, it's 30 percent of what my girl owes you. I'm home now. So I'll take care of the rest. She's out," D-Red stated.

"Whatever you say, Papi. Welcome back."

"Thank you," D-Red said, before walking out of the store.

When he got back from seeing his Probation Officer, he made love to Unique for hours. When they were sexually drained, they laid in each other's arms watching the news. Loco's face popped up on the screen.

"A 15-year-old Latino male is on the loose. He murdered Cito Cruz, a reputed stickup kid, as he tried to rob him and a few friends at a dice game. If you have seen this man, Police are asking that you call 860-718-TIPS.

"And yes, you may remain anonymous. The gunman's name is Edwin 'Loco' Torres," the news anchor said.

D-Red shook his head in a I told you so fashion, as he looked at Unique. She felt bad, because deep down inside she knew, if it wasn't for her, Loco would have never had to kill the stickup kid.

Chapter 29

Candy, Unique, and Melony sat in Unique's living room, listening to Hot 93.7, when a Destined to Blow Entertainment commercial came on.

"This ya boy, DJ Kid Fresh. And I'll be hosting the annual Destined to Blow Comedy Show, going down at the Bushnell Theater. The funny man, Mike Epps, Lil JJ, Martin Lawrence, Monique, and Tracy Morgan will all be in the building.

"So get ya tickets today at Anthony's Clothing, the Wreck Shop, and the Village, while they are still available," DJ Kid Fresh said, over the radio.

Unique turned down the radio with the remote.

"Y'all going to that comedy show," Unique asked.

"I ain't get my ticket yet," Candy replied.

"Mr. Ray Black said he got floor seats for all of us," Melony said.

"You serious?" Unique asked.

"Yeah, he's supposed to give them to me tonight, when I go over there."

"That's what's up. So how are things with you and him?"

"He is so incredible. I never thought I would find a man that could replace Brick City. But he proved me wrong," Melony stated.

Melony's phone rang, interrupting her conversation.

"Hello?" Melony said.

"Hey, sweetheart," Mr. Ray Black said.

"I was just talking about you. You're going to live a long time."

"As long as it's with you," Mr. Ray Black replied. Melony blushed.

"You know all the right things to say to a girl."

"I was brought up to be a gentleman."

"So, what's going on?" Melony asked.

"I was calling to ask you if you got the tickets to the concert. I dropped them in your mailbox."

"Hold on. Let me check."

Melony walked to her mailbox and found three front-row tickets to the Destined to Blow Concert.

"Thank you," Melony said.

"You're welcome. I won't be able to make it tonight. I have to fly out to Miami to promote my new artist, R&B Thug's, new album."

"When will you be back?"

"In a few days," Mr. Ray Black indicated.

"I'll miss you."

"I'll call every day."

"Okay, baby," Melony pouted.

"Bye."

Melony hung up the phone and gave Unique and Candy their tickets to the concert.

"I gotta get something cute to where to the concert, especially since we gone be in the front row," Unique said.

"Let's go to that new clothing store out in Bloomfield," Candy suggested.

"You mean Eblens?"

"Yeah, that's it."

"We can do that."

*   *   *

140

Silk and Ghetto drove down Main Street. Ghetto had been silent for the last couple of days. Silk knew him having to kill his own cousin was bothering him.

"What up, homey? You good?" Silk asked.

"Yeah, I'm cool," Ghetto replied.

Silk left it alone and pulled up on some street hustlers down in Chappelle Gardens, better known as Holly Wood.

"What up, Silk?" Fat Man asked.

"I need that bread," Ghetto replied.

"Shit been slow out here," Fat Man replied.

Ghetto looked at Fat Man. He had a smile on his face. Ghetto pulled out his .50 caliber handgun and jumped out of the car. Silk was right beside him with a .45 in-hand.

"You trying to play me?" Ghetto asked.

"Nah, man! I ain't trying to play you."

Ghetto went in Fat Man's pockets and pulled out a couple crumbled bills. He gritted his teeth before shooting him in the face. Silk clapped the other two kids in the head and chest, leaving no witness behind. They jumped back in the Cadillac truck and peeled off.

"Bum-ass nigga out here in the way!" Ghetto said, as he counted out the money he had just took from Fat Man. In all, he had $200.

*   *   *

The night of the Destined to Blow Comedy Show, everyone who was somebody was out dressed in their finest attire. It was a Grown & Sexy affair. Melony and her girls were definitely that. All eyes were on them, as

141

they walked into the Bushnell Theater. As they walked into the lobby, Candy bumped into Jerome.

"Hey, baby," Candy said.

"What's up, love? Where y'all sitting?

"We in the front row," Candy replied.

"How y'all pull that off? Those are better seats than I got. And the cat who's throwing this show is my man," Jerome replied.

"Mr. Ray Black hooked Melony up with some tickets."

"Will I see you later on?"

"For sure," Candy winked.

"All right, I know it's ladies' night. So I'll see you later."

"Bye, baby."

Jerome kissed Candy before walking off with his boys. Melony, Candy, and Unique walked to their seats. A few celebrities and Hartford's top elite criminal underworld shared the same row as them.

"Ooh, girl, look at Puff over there with Cassie," Unique said.

"Hey, Puff!" Melony yelled out.

Puffy looked their way and smiled. Cassie cut her eyes at Melony.

"Oh, no, she didn't!" Melony said.

"Girl, hush, the show is starting," Candy replied, as the lights got dim.

The first one out on the stage was Lil JJ. He did his thing and had the crowd laughing. Up next was funny man Mike Epps. He really had the crowd in stitches, as he cut on a few cats in the building. When

Martin came out, he had people out of their seats, dying laughing.

The crowd begged for more, and he gave them exactly what they wanted. And last, but not least, Monique came out and got on all the skinny bitches in the crowd. She had the crowd rolling, as she went in. At the end of the show, Unique, Melony, and Candy got autographs and took pictures with the comedians. Unique looked at her cell phone and saw D-Red's number pop up on the screen.

"Hello?" Unique said.

"Where you at?" D-Red asked.

"I'm dropping Candy and Melony off now. I'll be home in a minute."

"Don't wait up for me tonight."

"Why? What's up?" Unique inquired.

"I'm in the city handling some business. I won't be back until the morning."

D-Red hung up his phone. The girl in the passenger's seat of his whip sucked him off, as he drove down Tower Avenue, swerving in and out of lanes.

Chapter 30

Lil Crimey drove down Barbour Street with a jump-off named Cherry in the passenger's seat. Niggas was posted up in front of Corena's getting money when he pulled up.

"Go get me two Dutches," Lil Crimey told the girl.

Cherry grabbed the $2 from him and walked into the corner store. Red Rum stood up from the milk crates he was sitting on and walked over to the car.

"What up, Blood?" Red Rum asked.

"Ain't shit, bout to jump Cherry off."

"You heard about Fat Man, VA, and Antwon?"

"Nah, what happened?" Lil Crimey inquired.

"Them niggas got bodied last night."

"By who?"

"Niggas don't even know," Red Rum said, angrily.

Lil Crimey sucked his teeth and peeled off, right as Cherry was walking out of the store with the Dutch Masters. She frowned her face up, as she watched him pull off. The hustlers on the block laughed, as they tried to holla at her. She ignored their sexual advances and walked home to see if Lil Crimey, or one of her other niggas, would call.

*   *   *

Lil Crimey dipped up in Holly Wood. Low Life and Scumbag was in front of the building with a few other hustlers who were out on the block.

"What the fuck happened, Blood?" Lil Crimey asked, when he jumped out of the whip.

"Niggas killed Fat Man, VA, and Antwon in the project last night," Low Life said.

"Who?"

"Right now, niggas don't even know. But everybody got their ear to the streets trying to find out who pulled the trigger."

"Keep me posted, blood. You know we can't let this shit ride," Lil Crimey said.

"Word," Low Life replied, before Lil Crimey jumped back in the whip and peeled off.

*   *   *

D-Red sat parked on Belden Street talking to Camille on his cell phone, when the Narcs boxed him in with a Crown Victoria and a Ford Taurus. The Narcs jumped out, with guns drawn.

"Freeze! HPD!" Narcotics Officer Lefty yelled.

D-Red put his hands in the air. The Narcs snatched him out of his rental and searched him. They didn't find anything on him but a large wad of cash.

"Where did you get all this money?" Narcotics Officer Lefty asked.

"What money?" D-Red asked, trying to bribe the Narc.

Narcotics Officer Lefty searched the vehicle for drugs, but he was clean.

"What you doing in this drug area?"

"I was changing my CD, Officer," D-Red lied.

"Get out of here, and don't let me catch you out here no more tonight, or your ass is going down for trespassing."

D-Red jumped into his whip and pulled off $6500 less richer. The Narcs had split up the cash and was down the next block to harass more street hustlers. D-Red chalked up the loss and kept it moving. He knew things could have been worse, if they would have found the big eight he had in the stash box.

When he got to his crib on the south end, Unique was in the bedroom, dressed in a pair of boy shorts and wife beater. D-Red grabbed her by the waist and began to French kiss her. She kissed him back, as D-Red got her up out of her clothes.

He hit it doggy style, loving the way her ass clapped with every stroke. Unique moaned his name, as she felt him all up in her stomach. D-Red was putting that work in. Unique climaxed twice, before he skeeted all up in her.

"Ah, shit, baby! Here it comes!" D-Red said, right before shooting his load.

After he was done, he went to the bathroom and took a shower. He had a lot on his mind. Unique stepped into the shower with him and washed his body down. He returned the favor. When they were done, D-Red put on his robe and walked into the bedroom.

He turned the television to Sports Center and lit a blunt of Sour Diesel. He needed something to relax him. D-Red was tired of the harassment he received from the Police on a daily basis, and the haters who all wanted a piece of his hard-earned cash.

He began to think about giving the game up. He was already caked up and didn't need for nothing. But his addiction for the fast life wouldn't let him give the game up.

*   *   *

Calvin walked into the building on Belden Street. The snow was coming down outside, so he had his hands in his Polo Bubble Coat to keep him warm. As he walked down the hall, a kid pulled a black 9mm on him.

"You know what time it is, playboy! I need everything!" the stickup kid ordered.

"All right, little homey. Be easy with that hammer," Calvin said, before whipping out a .357 snub-nosed revolver and popping the kid in the forehead.

Off reflex, the stickup kid pulled the trigger and grazed Calvin in the neck. Calvin grabbed his neck before fleeing the scene, leaving the kid laying on the ground with blood leaking from his dome piece.

*   *   *

D-Red was laid up in the bed with Unique, when his phone started ringing.

"Hello?" D-Red said, in a sleepy voice.

"Where you at, homey? Shit just got real ugly in the hood," Calvin said.

"I'm in the house with my girl. You all right?"

"Yeah, but I need to holla at you."

"Where you at?" D-Red asked.

"I'm on Center Street."

"I'll be there in a few minutes."

"All right," Calvin replied.

When D-Red hung up with Calvin, Unique looked at him with concern in her eyes.

"Who was that?" Unique asked.

"That was Calvin. I gotta go holla at him."

"At this time of night? It's 3:00 a.m."

"I know. But he said the shit was urgent," D-Red indicated.

"Be careful, baby."

"All right."

D-Red kissed Unique before he got dressed and left the crib. He cocked back a 9mm and tucked the gun in his waistband before hopping out of his whip and walking into the building. When he stepped into the hallway, he saw his boy, Calvin, dressed in all black with a serious look on his face.

"What's up, Calvin?" D-Red asked.

"I had to murk some little nigga on the block."

"What happened?"

"The nigga tried to lay me down. So I let him have it," Calvin explained.

"Damn, you all right?"

"Yeah, I'm good. A bullet grazed me in the neck, but I'm straight."

"When I rode past Belden Street, the Police were still out there," D-Red stated.

"The hood gone be hot for a minute."

"Who was the nigga?"

"Man, I don't even know who he was. You know I don't be fucking with them little niggas," Calvin admitted.

"I already know."

"I just wanted to put you up on what's going on in the hood. Don't get caught slipping out there because shit is real."

"I'm heavy," D-Red replied, as he showed his boy his hammer.

"I'm about to take it in."

"All right, hit me on the hip if you need me," D-Red replied, before giving his boy dap and walking out of the building.

He looked up and down the block before pulling off.

Chapter 31

Base stood in front of his baby mother's house on the War Zone late night serving fiends. The block was banging, and he had just made a quick $600 in less than 20 minutes. Lil Crimey looked out his apartment window and saw Base on his block getting money.

He screwed up his face, because he felt disrespected. Base is taking food out of his mouth on the low. All the fiends knew to come to the building if nobody was outside. As Lil Crimey got dressed, Base walked into his apartment.

Lil Crimey had his .44 Magnum on him, as he stood on the War Zone waiting for Base to come back outside. Base is from Rice Heights Housing Projects and has only been given a pass to come through the War Zone because his brother, Tremain, is from Barbour Street.

And Lil Crimey is cool with him. But when it comes to cash, all that homey shit goes out the window. Base didn't come back outside that night. Lil Crimey was pissed off. He walked back into his crib and fucked Cherry until he fell asleep.

The next morning, Lil Crimey was up early. When he went outside, Base was on the block chilling with Red Rum, Real Deal, and Gutta. Lil Crimey walked up and gave everybody dap except Base.

"What up, Lil Crimey?" Base asked, as he held his hand out.

Lil Crimey looked at his hand like it was poisonous.

"You tell me, Blood!" Lil Crimey replied, with a mean mug on his face.

"What you talking about?" Base asked.

"What the fuck you doing on my block trying to get money?"

"Red Rum told me I could hustle out here."

"Red Rum don't run shit out here, Blood! This is my shit," Lil Crimey replied.

"Come on. It ain't even that serious. It's enough bread out here for everybody to eat."

"Nah, bra! Ain't no room out here! You got to go!"

"Oh, it's like that?" Base inquired.

"Hell, yeah, it's like that."

"I'll be back."

"What?" Lil Crimey asked, before he punched Base in the jaw.

Base snuffed Lil Crimey in the mouth. Red Rum, Gutta, and Red Deal jumped into the fight. They began to pound Base out on the sidewalk. Lil Crimey stomped base in the face with his Gore Tec Timberlands. Base managed to break loose from their brutal assault. He ran up Judson Street, lumped up with blood covering his face.

"Don't let me catch you out here no more!" Lil Crimey yelled up the block.

Base had caught Lil Crimey with a swift jab that had busted his bottom lip. Lil Crimey spit blood on the sidewalk.

"Word to Blood, I should have bodied that nigga," Lil Crimey said.

Red Rum leaned up against the fence with not much to say. Lil Crimey looked at him with anger in his eyes.

"What the fuck would make you tell him he can get money out here, Blood?" Lil Crimey asked.

"His brother's from the block. I figured it was cool."

"Man, we already got too many niggas out here who trying to eat. Ain't no room for nobody else," Lil Crimey replied.

"All right."

"Don't do that shit no more, Blood. If niggas ain't riding for this block when shit get real, they got to go! No more free lunches! Either you riding with us, or getting rode over."

*   *   *

D-Red sat at the kitchen table in the dope house bagging up heroin. His stamp, Gangster Lean, was booming and the fiends was chasing after that dope 100 miles per hour. A Puerto Rican woman named Betsy that D-Red went to school with walked into his dope house.

"D-Red, I need you, Papi," Betsy said.

"What's popping, Betsy?" D-Red asked.

"I need a bag of Gangster Lean so I can get off E."

"I ain't giving out testers right now."

"Please, Papi! I'm sick," Betsy pleaded.

"I need money right now."

"I'll suck your dick, Papi! That's what you like?" Betsy asked, as she began to look at him seductively.

152

"Betsy, get your ass out of here! Don't nobody want none of that stank cooch."

"Let me run some sales, Papi,"

"Here, Betsy, get your ass outside and run that money," D-Red said, as he passed her two bags of dope.

He knew she wouldn't stop until she got what she wanted. D-Red shook his head as he watched her shoot the heroin into her bloodstream. He remembered a time when he would have paid any amount of cash to have Betsy's lips around his dick. D-Red began to think back to the days when Betsy was one of the baddest bitches in the city.

*   *   *

Betsy stepped into Club 5.0 with her girls, Rosanne and Mariah. They were all wearing poom-poom shorts and wife beaters that showed off much cleavage. Betsy was the baddest bitch in the club and was feeling herself.

Niggas from all over was trying to get with her. But she was Goon Hands' girl. Goon Hands was a big-time dope dealer from Center Street. He drove around town in a cherry red Cadillac Fleetwood. His music in his car could be heard from blocks away.

You knew when he was coming, because he kept NWA in his tape deck. Goon Hands was a dappa street hustler who had a mean talk game. His pops was a pimp and instilled a lot of jewels in his son about the pimp game.

D-Red and Calvin stood at the bar, drinking champagne, when Goon Hands walked in with Betsy on his arm. At the time, D-Red was a small-time hustler in the game, but had dreams of getting it like Goon Hands.

"Yo, Betsy is a bad bitch," Calvin said.

"Yeah, she is. You think Goon Hands' tricking on her?" D-Red asked.

"You don't see all them jewels she rocking? I know you ain't think that shit just fell out of the sky? Hell, yeah, he setting that bread out."

"She got to be doing something to keep a nigga like Goon Hands' attention for so long. I'm gone hit that. Watch," D-Red said, as he eyed Betsy from across the room.

Calvin looked at him with doubt in his eyes. But D-Red stayed true to his words. A year later, Betsy had caught a dope habit from Goon Hands and began to come to the block for product when Goon Hands got bagged. D-Red caught her when she was fresh on the dope, before she got washed up.

"Betsy, what you doing out here?" D-Red asked, when he saw her in the hallway.

Betsy ran up to him and whispered in his ear.

"Baby, I need a couple bags of dope," Betsy said.

D-Red brought her up to his apartment. As soon as they walked inside, he started grabbing on her ass.

"Damn, that ass' chubby," D-Red said, with a smile on his face.

"You can't handle all this," Betsy replied, with a smile on her face.

"Yeah, okay. What you trying to get into?"

"Give me a couple of bags of dope to get my head right, and then you can show me what you working with," Betsy said, as she grabbed his dick through his sweatpants.

D-Red passed her three bags of dope. Betsy emptied the dope onto her glass mirror and Scar Faced all three bags.

"Slow down, girl. You gone kill ya self snorting all that shit up ya nose like that."

"I got this," Betsy replied, as she took off her coat and shirt.

She had the prettiest breasts D-Red had ever seen. He touched them gently before placing one in his mouth. Betsy moaned, as he sucked on her breast and unzipped her shorts. When she came out of her shorts, D-Red couldn't take his eyes off of her perfectly trimmed bush.

Betsy straddled him and began to ride him like a cowgirl. She was so tight and wet, D-Red felt like he was going to bust off prematurely. He flipped her on her back and began to stroke her nice and slow. He was making love to that pussy until he couldn't hold back any longer. D-Red skeeted all over her breast.

"Ah, shit! I'm cumming!" D-Red said, as he stroked his dick fast.

Betsy smiled, as she wiped his babies all over her lips. D-Red was turned out from the first episode. He began tricking with her on a daily basis for about a year, until she fell off completely and started shooting heroin. She was on the block tricking and wearing the same shit for weeks.

D-Red had to call it quits, but still looked out for her when he was out there. He always made sure she ate and had a place to stay. He had a few apartments on the block and gave her the keys to one of them that he used to bag up his dope. Besides the couch and table in the kitchen, the place was empty. D-Red knew not to leave anything of value in the apartment, because with a dope fiend, you never know.

*   *   *

D-Red was taken out of his thoughts when Betsy walked into the apartment.

"I got three sales outside. They all want bundles," Betsy said, as she dropped the cash on the table.

D-Red passed her three bundles.

"That's right, Betsy, get that money for daddy," D-Red said.

Betsy smiled, before walking back out the door.

*   *   *

When D-Red got into his house, it was 2:00 a.m. Unique walked into the living room, when he came in.

"You serious, D-Red? Every day, I have to come home to an empty bed? I'm getting tired of this shit," Unique said.

"Unique, what the hell you talking about?"

"You never home anymore. It's the same shit every night. Me, alone, in this apartment."

"You know what's up. I'm out getting money," D-Red replied, as he opened his safe and stacked some cash in the safe.

"You think I'm stupid, D-Red? I know you got bitches on the side."

"Unique, you the only woman who I'll ever have eyes for. What I want with them other women when I got your fine chocolate ass at home?" D-Red asked, before grabbing her by the waist and pulling her close to him.

He looked her in the eyes.

"Unique, I love you and wouldn't fuck up what we got for nothing in the world. I'm finally happy, for once in my life."

"If you love me, why do you neglect me?"

"I'll never neglect you, baby," D-Red said, before they started tongue-kissing.

The teddy Unique was wearing had D-Red horny as hell. He bent her over the kitchen table and hit it from the back until he got his little man out the streets.

Chapter 32

Lil Crimey, Real Deal, Gutta, and Red Rum sat on the porch, listening to 50 Cent, when a black Nissan Maxima came through the block busting off mad shots. They hit the floor, as shots came in their direction. Base was hanging out of the window, as he banged off a .45 automatic. When the shots stopped, Lil Crimey and his team jumped up with their hammers out.

"Who the fuck was that?" Red Rum asked.

"That was that nigga, Base!" Gutta replied.

"I'm gone murder that nigga."

"Tremain was driving," Real Deal added.

"Both of them niggas gone get touched! Ride through Barbour Street," Lil Crimey said, as he jumped in the backseat of his truck.

They pulled off and drove down Barbour Street. A few niggas was standing in the cut on the side of Blues package store. Lil Crimey rolled his window down.

"Yo, who was that dumping on the War Zone?" Scumbag asked.

"That was Tremain and Base. They just tried to get right on us."

"I just saw them niggas drive down Barbour, too. I wish I would have known that. I would have aired that shit out, Blood."

"Tremain gotta come home," Lil Crimey insinuated.

"Word to Blood."

*　　*　　*

Tremain and Base sat parked on the Deuce in front of Block's house. Block came out of the crib and walked up to the car.

"What's good, Kik?" Block asked.

"Ain't shit. I just had to get right on niggas from the War Zone."

"You beefing with them niggas, too?"

"Yeah," Base admitted.

"I thought ya baby mother live out there, Base?"

"She do."

"How you gone work that out?" Block inquired.

"I gotta stay strapped."

"Me and my niggas is beefing hard with them niggas. Word to the Gods, it's been on sight every time we bump heads."

"Them niggas jumped me. So I'm trying to rock all them niggas to sleep," Base declared.

"You sure you ready to go all out?"

"I was born ready."

"Then let's boost the murder rate."

*   *   *

Melony and Mr. Ray Black stood at the roulette wheel in Fox Woods Casino.

"Let me get $100 on black," Melony said.

Her bet was taken right before the roulette wheel was spun.

"Black," the dealer said, when the ball stopped on black.

159

Melony jumped up and down in excitement, when she realized she had won. After she was given her chips, she hugged Mr. Ray Black.

"Congratulations, baby! You won," Mr. Ray Black said.

"Thank you, baby," Melony replied.

"Where do you want to go next?"

"Let's go to the slot machines," Melony suggested.

"Do ya thing, baby. But I think I'm a little too grown for the slot machines. I'll be at the blackjack table," Mr. Ray Black replied.

"Whatever," Melony said, with a smile on her face.

Mr. Ray Black kissed her on the lips before they parted ways. It didn't take Melony long to burn through her winnings. When she was out of cash, she met back up with Mr. Ray Black. They enjoyed a jazz concert before going back up to their room to enjoy a candle lit dinner for two. Melony hadn't been this happy in a while. And she didn't want the moment to ever end.

*   *   *

Silk and Ghetto sat at the bar in Main & Tower drinking cognac, when Heat Holder walked in. He gave the killers head nods, when he walked inside. They acknowledged Heat Holder.

"What's up, Heat Holder?" Silk asked, with a smile on his face.

"Ain't shit. You know ya boy just touched down."

"Word?"

"Yeah, them crackers had a nigga up in them mountains for a year," Heat Holder admitted.

"I thought you was just laying low."

"Nah, I got bagged for a parole violation. I'm off papers now. So I'm good."

"Where you hustling at?" Silk inquired.

"I ain't get my hands on nothing yet. But, shit, you know me. It won't be long before I'm up again."

"You strapped?" Ghetto echoed.

"Nah."

"I got something for you. Walk me out to the car."

Heat Holder followed Silk out to his whip. Silk passed his boy a .38 snub-nosed revolver and a stack of dope.

"This is a little something to get you back to where you need to be."

"Good looking, homey. Ya boy needed this. My ribs is touching right now."

"Come see me on Bed Roc. I might got some real work for you," Silk instructed him.

"All right, you got a number?"

Silk passed him a business card with his phone number on it.

"Get at me, Heat Holder. You know we go back since Camp Courant days."

"I already know," Heat Holder replied, with a smile on his face.

He gave his boy dap before walking back in the bar. Silk and Ghetto left the bar drunk and high off lamb spread and Remy Martin.

"It's crazy how niggas from Brook Street ain't look out for the homey when he came home," Silk said.

"You know how the hood is, every man for his self."

161

"Niggas around the way ain't shit."
"I could have told you that."

Chapter 33

<u>Candy</u>

Candy grew up in West Brook Housing Projects. As a youth, she was enrolled in the Project Concern Program. But that didn't last long. A white girl had called her a nigger and she just lost it. Candy beat the girl up so bad she was black-and-blue for weeks.

Candy got kicked out of the Project Concern Program indefinitely, and it was back to the hood she went. Candy didn't care, though, because she was right back in school with all of her friends. Her first week back in Lewis Fox Middle School, she was right back in the mix of things. As she sat in her homeroom class with Unique and Melony, Unique spoke her mind.

"Candy, what happened? I thought you was in the Project Concern Program," Unique said.

"I was. But some white bitch called me out of my name. So I beat her ass and they kicked me out."

"They kicked you out for that?"

"Yeah, they didn't even want to hear my side of the story," Candy huffed.

"Them crackers make they own rules," Curtis said.

"Boy, where you come from?" Unique asked.

"I heard the sister say she was called out of her name when she was out there in the suburbs. You need to notify the NAACP and inform them about these unjust laws out there in Whitey Ville," Curtis said.

"Nah, it ain't even that serious. I already beat that bitch's ass. So she'll know not to disrespect another black person."

Unique cut into the conversation.

"Y'all trying to get high? I got some of that Arizona mixed with hash."

"Hell, yeah," Candy replied.

Unique, Candy, and Melony walked towards the door.

"Where are you three going?" Professor Dean asked.

"To the bathroom," they replied, in unison.

Professor Dean went back to teaching the class. When the girls got to the bathroom, Unique pulled out the blunt and sparked it. She hid the weed behind her back when the door opened. Curtis walked in.

"Boy, what you doing in here? This is the girls' bathroom," Unique said.

"Pass that. I'm trying to get high," Curtis replied.

Unique took a few pulls off the blunt before passing it around. When the blunt got to Candy, the door opened again. Ms. Robinson walked into the bathroom. Candy dropped the blunt on the floor.

"What is going on in here? I smell marijuana. Were you four in here smoking?" Ms. Robinson asked.

"No, ma'am," they all said in unison.

"All of you in my office! Now!" Ms. Robinson demanded.

When Candy was seen by the Principal, she was given the longest speech.

"Candy, I'm so disappointed in you. Don't you know when you blow an opportunity to do better in life, you don't only kill an opportunity for yourself, but for black people in a whole? We were rooting for you to win. And you let everyone down.

"And now, you're back in my school smoking marijuana in the bathroom like you have no home training. What do you have to say for yourself?"

"If I was given the opportunity to go back into the past, I wouldn't change a thing. I have no regrets, and was brought up to respect those who respect me. I wasn't taught to turn the other cheek. You either gone respect me and what I believe in, or I'm gone make you respect me."

Ms. Robinson suspended Candy, but couldn't do anything but respect the statement she had just made. When Candy got home, her mother spassed out on her.

"What the hell is wrong with you, Candy? First you get kicked out of the Project Concern Program. And now, I hear you're smoking weed in school. What are you trying to be, a bum for the rest of your life?"

"No."

"Well, if you don't straighten up, that's exactly what you gone be! A damn bum! And I don't got no time to be trying to take care of no bums, Candy! I'm telling you now. Keep messing up in school! I'm gone kick yo ass out on the streets."

Candy was not in the mood for her mother's threats today. She walked up to her room and dialed up Unique's phone number.

"Hello," Unique said.

"What up, girl? What you doing?"

"Chilling, braiding my little cousin's hair."

"My mother is in here, tripping," Unique complained.

"Mine's, too, but I ain't really trying to hear what she talking about. You going to Brenda's house party?"

"My mother ain't letting me go nowhere."

"I heard the party supposed to be like that," Unique explained.

"I wish I could go."

"Girl, sneak out when she go to sleep."

"I'm already in enough trouble," Candy scoffed.

"What more could she do to you? You're already on punishment."

"What time does the party start?

"8:00 p.m.," Unique informed her.

"I'll meet you in the back at 7:45 p.m."

"All right."

Candy hung up the phone and walked down the stairs. Her mother was in the kitchen fixing dinner.

"You hungry?" her mother asked, when she walked into the kitchen.

"A little," Candy replied.

Her mother fixed them both a plate of food.

"Candy, I know you might think I be hard on you. But I only want the best for you. I don't want you to end up like me, 40 years old with an 8th-grade education, dead broke, and living in the projects for the rest of your life. Candy, you deserve better and I'm gone make sure you get better."

"I know, mama."

Candy and her mother enjoyed dinner together, before her mother went up to her bedroom to watch *Living Single*. Candy wasted no time sneaking out. She grabbed a bunch of pillows and placed them under the covers to look like she was in her bed, sleeping.

"What took you so long?" Unique asked.

"My mother had me in there, talking me to death," Candy replied.

"Come on, let's go. Melony is waiting on us at the party."

When they got to the basement party, reggae music was blasting through the speakers. Unique slid off to a corner of the club with D-Red. Melony and a kid name C-Mack, was on the dance floor, getting they dance on. Candy was standing by herself, when Rondell walked up to her.

"You want to dance?" Rondell asked.

Candy looked at Rondell and liked what she saw. He was a sharp dresser and kept his self well-groomed.

"I don't feel like dancing."

"Well, maybe we can get to know each other a little better. I'm Rondell."

Rondell stuck his hand out.

"I'm Candy."

"Nice to meet you, Candy."

Rondell held her hand, as he looked into her baby brown eyes and got lost.

"So, where you from, Rondell?" Candy asked, as she pulled her hand out of his grasp.

"I'm from Bowles Park."

"I never saw you out there before."

"My family just moved out there. I'm originally from East Hartford," Rondell stated.

"So, how you like it out here?"

"It's cool. I been coming to Hartford before I moved, though. I got family all through Hartford."

"Did you start school yet out here?" Candy asked.

167

"My aunt's letting me use her address in East Hartford until the end of the school year. And then, I'm transferring out here."

"Well, here come my girls. So I guess I'll see you around."

Rondell passed her his phone number.

"Here's my number. Give me a call sometime," Rondell suggested.

"I'll do that," Candy replied, with a smile on her face.

Melony and Unique walked over.

"Who was that?" Unique asked.

"Just some boy," Candy replied.

"He's cute," Melony added.

Candy smiled.

"So, what's the deal with him?" Unique asked.

"He just moved out here from East Hartford."

"So, you gone holla at him?"

"I might," Candy whispered.

"Y'all will make a cute couple."

Candy smiled. Unique sparked a blunt of weed. She took a few pulls off the weed before trying to pass it to Candy.

"Nah, I'm good," Candy said.

"What's wrong?" Unique asked.

"I don't feel like smoking," Candy replied.

"All right," Unique said, as she passed the weed to Melony.

Candy knew she was already disobeying her mother's orders by sneaking out of the house. She didn't want to make things worse by smoking weed again. At the end of the party, Candy snuck back in the house. But she didn't get upstairs before her mother flicked on the lights.

"You think you're so slick, Candy! Did I tell you that you could leave this house?" her mother asked.

"No, mama."

"And you been smoking again, haven't you?"

"No," Candy insisted.

"Don't lie to me, Candy."

"I haven't."

"Then, why it smell like you just came from a Bob Marley concert?" her mother pressed on.

"They were smoking at the party, and it got on my clothes."

"I hope you enjoyed it, because you won't be leaving this house anytime soon. And that phone and television that used to be in your room is gone. From now on, you gone work for everything you want. You think you grown. Well, I'm gone treat you like you grown! Now, get the hell out of my face!"

Candy walked to her room and sucked her teeth. Her phone, television, and videogames were all gone, and she was left with four walls to stare at. Candy laid down in her bed and fell asleep from boredom. Her punishment lasted for 30 days before she was able to get her phone, television, and videogames back.

Her curfew had gone from 8:00 p.m. to 6:00 p.m. When she finally got a chance to call Rondell, she was informed that he was locked up for selling weed. His brother gave her the address to the Juvenile Center on Broad Street.

She wrote Rondell on a regular basis and sent him pictures. Rondell had respected that she hadn't forgotten

169

about him. They became a couple. And when Rondell came home from doing a bid in Long Lane, she gave him her virginity.

Things were good between them for a few years. When Candy turned 18, she got her own apartment. She let Rondell move in with her, and that's when she began to see his possessive ways. He would beat on her whenever he felt like it, over any little thing, and cheat with different women.

When Candy found out about his cheating ways, she kicked him to the curb. But Rondell was obsessed with her, and wasn't giving up on their relationship that easy.

Chapter 34

Lil Crimey and his mob of Bloods stood in the back of Tremain's house on Barbour Street with guns out. He hadn't been home in two days and niggas was getting antsy.

"Where these niggas at, Blood?" Lil Crimey asked.

"You think them niggas is hiding?" Gutta asked.

"You know, them niggas is ducking that rec! This is what the fuck I do! I play with them bangers," Lil Crimey replied, as he clutched a 10mm handgun.

"Let's get out of here," Gutta said.

Just as the words left his mouth, Tremain's burgundy Honda Accord pulled into the backyard with the system bumping *Reasonable Doubt*. Lil Crimey and his mob got low, as Tremain jumped out of his whip with his daughter. Gutta was about to get up when Lil Crimey stopped him.

"Nah, Blood, not now. He got his seed with him. Let him live," Lil Crimey ordered.

Gutta reluctantly followed his boy's orders.

*   *   *

Biggie Smalls' *Ready to Die* album bumped in Tremain's room, as he smoked on a blunt of purple haze and watched a Smack DVD. Keisha walked into the room in nothing but her t-shirt and panties. Tremain admired his baby mother, as she held his two-year-old daughter in her hands.

His daughter was the splitting image of her mother, and he loved them both dearly. His daughter reached for him. Tremain shook his head, no.

"Stay with your mother. Keisha, why you got her in here while I'm smoking?" Tremain asked.

"She was asking for you."

Tremain shook his head, because his baby mother could be so stupid at times.

"Bring her in the other room. I'll be in there in a minute."

Keisha walked to her daughter's room and placed her inside of the playpen. Tremain watched Dip Set spit gangster lyrics on the Smack DVD. Moments later, his phone started ringing. The number was blocked, but he answered anyway.

"Hello," Tremain said.

"Word to Blood, I'm gone slump you out here on these streets," Lil Crimey said.

"You know where I'm at," Tremain replied, as he clutched the Desert Eagle that rested on his lap.

"I gave you a pass tonight. I ain't want no blood to get on my God daughter."

Tremain's whole facial expression changed, as he peeked out the window with his gun in-hand.

"Don't get scared now. I ain't gone kill you tonight. But tomorrow's another day," Lil Crimey replied before hanging up.

*   *   *

Jerome drove down Albany Avenue with Candy in the passenger's seat. It was a nice day outside, and he was stunting through the city in a brand-new Lincoln Navigator. He pulled up in front of Bernice's.

"You hungry, Bay?" Jerome asked.

"Yeah, get me the steak, rice and peas, and plantains dinner with a golden champagne."

Jerome went inside and ordered their food. He saw his boy, Javon, in front of the store, when he walked out.

"Jerome, what's up, playboy?" Javon asked.

"Ain't shit. What's up with you?"

"I'm out here doing my numbers. I'm trying to get some work, but shit's dry in the hood right now."

"How much work you was trying to copp?" Jerome inquired.

"A bird, what's the price?"

"Twenty-two thousand."

"Word?" Javon questioned.

"Yeah, and it's fish scale."

"You got it on you now?"

"Nah, meet me on ya block in 10 minutes," Jerome instructed.

"All right."

Jerome gave his boy dap before hopping In his whip and pulling off. He went to Candy's apartment out in West Brook and told her to grab a bird for him. Candy put the drugs in her purse and walked back outside. When she hopped back in the whip, she passed the drugs to Jerome. He met up with Javon on Lenox Street and served him.

"Kik, if this shit is fire, I'm gone be calling," Javon said.

"Oh, it's definitely fire. Watch how ya phone be ringing when you flood the streets with that."

Javon gave Jerome dap before he pulled off. Jerome made a few more stops before they went to his penthouse to hang out. He sparked a blunt and put in a DVD called *Statistic*. Candy cuddled up next to him, as they watched the movie together.

Since they had been together, Jerome had introduced her to a lifestyle she wasn't accustomed to. Jerome made sure Candy was well-taken care of. He treated her like royalty, and Candy loved him for that.

Chapter 35

Tremain walked to the corner store on Barbour Street. He grabbed a pack of Pull-Ups and a can of Juicy Juice from the freezer. He placed the items on the counter.

"Is that it?" Poppi asked.

"Let me get a turkey grinder," Tremain replied.

As Poppi fixed his grinder, the bells on the door rang. Tremain pulled out his Desert Eagle when he saw C-Bo from the War Zone walk into the store.

"Yo, chill! I ain't have nothing to do with that shit between you and Lil Crimey," C-Bo said.

"Leave my store!" Poppi ordered, as he reached for his gun under the counter.

Tremain grabbed his stuff and walked out the store with his gun still drawn on C-Bo. C-Bo had his hands in the air, as Tremain backpedaled out of the store. He was pissed that he let Tremain get the drop on him like that.

Any other time, he would never leave the crib without his banger. The night before, he had tossed it when the Narcs chased him on the block. He called up Lil Crimey ASAP.

* * *

Lil Crimey sat parked on Naugatuck Street, rolling a Dutch Master, when he got a call from C-Bo on his cell phone.

"Hello," Lil Crimey said.

"Yo, this nigga, Tremain, just pulled a banger on me! Where you at?"

"I just left out the corner store. I'm walking down there right now. Don't go nowhere."

"All right."

When C-Bo got to Naugatuck, he saw Lil Crimey sitting in a Honda CRX. He jumped in the passenger's seat of his whip.

"This nigga gotta get slumped, Blood!" C-Bo said.

"Why you ain't dump on that nigga?" Lil Crimey asked.

"The Narcs chased me last night. I had to toss my banger."

"You ain't go back for it?"

"Yeah, but that shit was gone. Somebody must have saw when I tossed it."

Lil Crimey went into the glove box and passed C-Bo a black 9mm.

"Good looking, Blood."

"Ain't nothing."

Lil Crimey sparked a blunt and pulled off. He drove past Tremain's house, but he wasn't outside.

"I should spray that shit up," C-Bo said.

"Nah, be easy. We will catch him," Lil Crimey replied.

C-Bo took a pull off the blunt and leaned back in the passenger's seat.

*　　*　　*

Tremain chilled on the Deuce with Block and his brother, Base. The block was banging early morning, and they was out there getting it.

"Kik, guess who I saw today," Tremain said.

176

"Who?" Blocked asked.

"C-Bo. I pulled the banger out on that nigga and he started copping pleads and shit," Tremain said.

"You should have clapped him. C-Bo a grimy nigga and can't be trusted."

"If Poppi ain't have that shit on camera, I definitely would have peeled his fruit."

"Niggas know when I come through! Niggas are dying," Block said.

"I'm trying to go through there tonight."

"Nah, fall back. I'll let you know when it's time to get right."

Chapter 36

D-Red pulled up at the carwash on Homestead Avenue. Car Wash ran up to his car, when he saw him.

"Neph, let me wash the car," Car Wash said.

"Clean my shit inside and out," D-Red said, before jumping out of the whip with a half-smoked blunt between his lips.

"I got you, neph."

D-Red got a bunch of quarters and paid for the machine. He stood on the side as Car Wash did his thing. A bad-ass red-boned chick named Shelly came walking up Homestead with her girls.

"Yo!" D-Red called out.

Shelly turned around to see who was calling her. When she saw who it was, she stopped.

"What's up?" Shelly asked.

"Come here," D-Red replied.

"You come here."

D-Red walked over to the girl.

"What's ya name, ma?"

"Shelly."

"You got a man, Shelly?" D-Red inquired.

"Nah."

"You trying to chill with me tonight?"

"We can do that," Shelly stated, smiling.

"You want to give me your phone number?"

"I'm out of minutes right now. But you can give me yours."

D-Red went in his pocket, pulled out a large wad of cash, and handed the girl $20.

"Go buy some minutes. I'll be right here when you get back."

"All right."

D-Red sat on the large bricks and watched Shelly walk into the store. She had a banging body, and D-Red couldn't wait to see what that box was hitting on. When the girl came out of the store, she had her number written on a piece of paper for him.

"Call me in an hour," Shelly said.

"All right."

D-Red tucked the number in his pocket before relighting his blunt and calling his sales back. He caught a few dope sales at the carwash before pulling off in his Benz. When he got to Belden Street, a couple of his little niggas was on the block.

"Yo, come in the hallway," D-Red said.

The two hustlers followed him into the hallway.

"What's up?" Youngster asked.

"Y'all little niggas strapped out here?"

"All day," the boys replied, as they showed D-Red the twin .38 revolvers that he had bought for them when they first got in the game.

"Y'all be easy out here. Niggas be trying to come through the block and lay niggas down."

"They try that shit when I'm out here, and it's gone get ugly," Freddy replied.

"that's what I'm talking about. Y'all niggas hold this shit down. I'm out," D-Red replied.

"I need five stacks," Youngster said.

D-Red pulled the dope from out of his inside jacket pocket and handed it to Youngster.

"Let me get the same thing," Freddy said.

179

D-Red served them and walked into his apartment on the block. He turned on the television to Sports Center and cracked a bottle of Remy Martin before calling Shelly. She answered on the second ring.

"Hello?" Shelly said.

"What up?"

"I'm chilling. I just got in the house."

"Where you live at?" D-Red asked.

"On Acton Street."

"Can I come check you?"

"Yeah, you can do that," Shelly replied.

"I'm on my way. What number Acton?"

"79 Acton Street."

"All right."

D-Red left out the apartment and jumped in his Benz. He had *Juice* playing on the television screen, as he drove through the hood. When he got to Acton Street, he saw a bunch of niggas from the project standing outside.

He hit the horn before pulling into her driveway. Shelly came out and signaled for D-Red to come inside. D-Red hesitated for a minute. He wasn't trying to get caught slipping in other niggas' hoods. When he saw his man, Moet, out there, he felt a little more relaxed.

"D-Red, what up, baby?" Moet asked.

"What's good, Moet?" D-Red said, as he gave him dap.

"Where you going?"

"Up in Shelly's crib."

"I'm out here. Holla at me later," Moet stated.

"All right."

D-Red stepped into Shelly's house. As soon as he walked through the door, he wasn't feeling it at all. She had a bunch of little niggas in the crib, and they were eyeing D-Red as he walked into her room.

"Who all them little niggas in your crib?" D-Red asked.

"My brother's friends. Don't trip. You good," Shelly said.

"Lock that door."

Shelly locked her door. D-Red twisted up a blunt and sparked it. He took a few deep pulls before passing the weed to Shelly. They played tennis with the blunt until it was gone. D-Red got closer to Shelly. He began to feel on her breasts, as he kissed on her juicy red lips.

Shelly kissed him back, as she unzipped his pants and started stroking his dick. She had D-Red open and he was loving it. When he was ready to go, he bent Shelly over the bed and started hitting it doggy style. With every stroke, her pussy made a farting noise.

She was hot and wet, as D-Red beat it up. When he couldn't hold back any longer, he skeeted into the Rough Rider condom he was wearing.

"Ah, shit!" D-Red said, as he reached his climax.

He grabbed a towel off the door and cleaned his self off.

"Shelly, I gotta go," D-Red said.

"Let me walk you to the door," Shelly said, as she cleaned herself off, as well.

D-Red and Shelly walked to the door. The little niggas who was in the living room were now on the front porch. Shelly kissed D-Red on the lips.

"Call me later," Shelly said.

"All right."

D-Red walked out of the crib and began to walk towards his car. He was about a foot away from the car, when a man dressed in all black with a ski mask on his face ran up on him with a .357 revolver pointed in his face.

"Nigga, you know what it is! Come up off everything," the stickup kid said.

"Fuck!" D-Red said out loud.

The stickup kid twisted his gun sideways.

"I said run everything."

D-Red took his cash out of his pocket and handed it to the stickup kid.

Here you go, player. You can have all this shit. This ain't about nothing," D-Red said.

The stickup kid snatched the cash and ran. D-Red pulled out a black 9 and started busting at the stickup kid. He missed, but the gun made a lot of noise and scared the kids off who were standing on the porch. D-Red jumped in his whip and peeled off. When he got back to his block, Calvin was out there.

"D-Red, what's up?"

"I just got robbed," D-Red said.

"What? By who?"

"I don't know. Some kid wearing a ski mask pulled a gun on me and took some cash."

"How much he get?" Calvin asked.

"About $600."

"This shit is crazy."

"I shot at him, but he got away," D-Red huffed.

"Who was you going to see on Acton Street?

"Some little jump I just met."

"You sure she didn't set you up?"

"That's a good question," D-Red stated, suspiciously.

*   *   *

C-Bo crept up in Shelly's apartment when he got a chirp from her telling him that D-Red had left. She was laying in the bed, under the sheets, topless.
C-Bo sat on her bed and counted the cash he had just got from D-Red. He passed her $200 and cuffed the rest.

"That's all he had? That nigga had a grip on him, when I saw him earlier," Shelly said.

"I should've patted the nigga down. I think he held out on me."

"You ain't pat him down? What the hell is wrong with you? You got a death wish or something?"

C-Bo ignored her last question and slid under the sheet.

"You gave that nigga any pussy?" C-Bo asked.

"You know this is yours and only yours, daddy."

"That's right," C-Bo said, as he began to rub up and down on her thighs and breasts.

*   *   *

D-Red called Shelly on his Nextel phone. She answered on the second ring.

"Hello?" Shelly said.

"Bitch, you set me up!" D-Red asked.

"What? I would never do that! D-Red, what are you talking about?"

183

"I got robbed when I left your house and I think you set me up."

"D-Red, baby, I was worried sick when my brother told me you were shooting at whoever robbed you. If you hadn't called me blocked, I would have called to see if you were okay."

"I'm good," D-Red replied.

"So, what happens with us?"

"I can't fuck with you, Shelly. That shit was mad suspect today."

"D-Red, I swear on my life that I had nothing to do with you getting robbed," Shelly lied through her teeth.

"Don't let me see you in the streets, bitch. I'm gone make my girl beat your ass!" D-Red said.

"Fuck you, nigga!" Shelly yelled into the phone, right before hanging up.

D-Red wasn't for certain that she had anything to do with the robbery. That was the only reason he didn't shoot up her house. D-Red chalked the loss up and made a promise to move smarter on the streets.

Chapter 37

Block, Tremain, and Base pulled up at the drive-thru at McDonald's on the Ave. As they waited for their orders, a black Cadillac pulled on the side of them, boxing them in. Lil Crimey hung out the passenger's side with his hood and ski mask over his face, as he started busting off shots.

Block ducked under the seat, but Tremain and Base weren't so lucky. The first two slugs hit Base in the face. And the next three bullets tore into Tremain's forehead, killing him instantly. Red Rum stepped on the gas, peeling out of the parking lot. Block jumped out of the backseat and took off on foot down the Avenue.

*   *   *

Nashelle and her girls were standing on the War Zone, when a black Honda Accord drove through the block. Block and Prada shot at niggas who were on the block, but Daniel ended up getting shot in the head. Nashelle screamed, as she watched her friend on the ground, fighting for her life.

"Daniel, please don't die on me, girl! Somebody call 911," Nashelle yelled out, as tears ran down her face.

*   *   *

Detective Jennings and Detective Brenton pulled up on the War Zone. Over 22 shell casings laid on the ground.

185

"What we got here?" Detective Brenton asked a female Officer.

"Daniel Sullivan, a 22-year-old black woman, was dead on arrival," the Officer explained.

"Do we have any witnesses?"

"One, but she's not trying to speak with us in front of everyone."

"Have a cab drive her to the station."

*   *   *

Nashelle sat in the Police Station on Jennings Road with tears in her eyes. Detective Brenton passed her a napkin.

"Thank you, Detective," Nashelle said.

"No problem. I heard the victim was a close friend of yours."

"My best friend! Daniel didn't deserve to die the way she did."

"Who killed her?" Detective Brenton inquired.

"Jeffrey Maddox aka Block. He be on Cabot Street."

"Why was your friend murdered?"

"My neighborhood and their neighborhood are beefing," Nashelle informed him.

"We know about the War Zone and A.V.E. beef. But do you think the bullet was meant for her?"

"No, it was some boys out there that they were shooting at."

"I'm going to need you to write everything down for me," Detective Brenton directed.

"All right."

*   *   *

Block slept in his crib on Cabot Street with his baby mother, when the Police kicked his door down with guns drawn, at 4:00 a.m. They placed him in handcuffs and read him his rights, before booking him for murder. When Block went in front of the Judge and his bond was raised to $500,000 cash, he knew he was all set.

Even if niggas had that type of bread to put up for Block, the Feds would snatch him up for posting that type of bond.

Chapter 38

D-Red drove down Mather Street early morning, when Seven Thirty flagged him down. D-Red pulled over. Seven Thirty jumped in the passenger's seat.

"What up, boy?" D-Red asked.

"I need a stack. I gotta get this money," Seven Thirty said, as he passed D-Red $250.

"You just came out?" D-Red asked.

"Yeah, I was up early in Daphny's crib getting sucked off. Bra, her head game is vicious," Seven Thirty said.

D-Red gritted his teeth as Seven Thirty bragged about getting head from his side chick. As soon as he served Seven Thirty, he pulled in front of Daphny's crib and went upstairs. He knocked on the door.

"Who is it?" Daphny asked, with an attitude.

"It's me! Open the door!" D-Red demanded.

Daphny opened the door.

"What the hell wrong with you beating on my door like that? Somebody's chasing you?"

D-Red slapped her with the black side of his hand.

"Bitch, what the fuck is wrong with you fucking niggas in the crib I pay rent for?" D-Red asked, as he stood over Daphny with his chest heaving up and down.

"D-Red, get the hell out of my house before I call the cops!"

"What, bitch?" D-Red said, before he began to choke her out.

Daphny's light-skinned face turned red, as she gasped for air.

"I will kill you if I ever hear you talking about calling the cops on me again!" D-Red said, before letting her go.

Daphny grabbed her neck, as she caught her breath. She had a frightened look on her face. D-Red walked over to her.

"Get up," D-Red said.

Daphny backed away from him in fear.

"I'm sorry, all right. Now, get up off the floor," D-Red said, as he helped her off the ground.

Tears ran down her face, as D-Red helped her off the ground. She was only wearing a bra and panties. D-Red was horny as hell. He started kissing her, but she pushed away.

"No! Stop!" Daphny said.

D-Red pushed her onto the couch, ripped her panties off, and began to savagely rape her.

Tears ran down Daphny's face, as she regretted getting herself involved in this fucked-up situation.

*   *   *

Their secret love affair started three years ago. Daphny is Unique's cousin and would often come through to check her cousin, Unique. One day, D-Red was the only one there, and he invited her inside to wait for Unique.

They had a few drinks, as they chilled and watched music videos. D-Red kissed Daphny on the lips. She pulled back.

"What are you doing?" Daphny asked.

"I want you," D-Red replied.

189

"But you with my cousin. I can't do that."

"I'll take you shopping. You can have whatever you like," D-Red replied.

Dollar signs ran through Daphny's head, as she gave in to D-Red. They had sex all over the crib for hours. Unique was out-of-town with Melony and Candy. They had left for the All-Star game that morning. D-Red had known this information, and hadn't bothered to tell Daphny.

From that day on, they were sleeping together on a regular basis. But now Daphny was starting to regret ever dealing with him.

Chapter 39

Animal Cuz stepped on Murda Field in a wife beater, Polo jeans, and a fresh pair of wheat brown Timberland boots. He was chiseled up something serious from working out on a daily basis, and eating healthy, while he was on lock. Animal Cuz had been gone for two years.

"Animal Cuz, what's up, Kik? When you get out?" Stretch asked.

"They let me out today."

"My Kik back out here! We about to get this paper," Stretch said, excitedly.

"What's up with Daphny?"

Stretch shook his head.

"Man, Kik, she out here jumping like crazy."

Animal Cuz wasn't surprised by the news. He had been gone for two years and didn't expect her to wait for him.

"I need to go see my seed."

"She's still living on the block."

"I'll be back," Animal Cuz stated.

"Here go a little something until you get back on ya feet," Stretch said, as he passed Animal Cuz a small knot of cash and a half-ounce of crack.

"Good looking, Kik."

Animal Cuz tucked the cash and drugs in his Polo jeans, before walking into the building. The stench of marijuana was strong in the air, as he walked down the dark hallway. When he got to Daphny's apartment, he knocked on the door. She opened the door and was surprised when she saw Animal Cuz.

191

"Justin, when did you get out?" Daphny asked, calling him by government name.

"I came home today. Is Ashley here?"

"Yeah, she's in her room," Daphny replied, as she looked him up and down.

"You gone let me in?"

Animal Cuz walked past his baby mother and went straight to his daughter's room. She was in her room playing with her dolls.

"Hey, baby girl," Animal Cuz said.

"Daddy!" Ashley yelled.

She jumped to her feet and ran over to her father. Animal Cuz picked his daughter up and hugged her tightly.

"What's up, baby girl?"

"I'm glad you're home, daddy! Mommy has been real sad since you been gone."

"Why has she been sad, baby?" Animal Cuz inquired, concerned.

"Some mean guy hits her."

"What? Does he hit you?"

"No."

Animal Cuz gritted his teeth, as he put his daughter down and walked into the living room.

"What nigga you got around my daughter who be beating on you?" Animal Cuz asked.

"Let it go, Justin."

"Nah, fuck that! Who is this nigga?"

D-Red walked out of the backroom.

"You better listen to your baby mother if you know what's good for you," D-Red said.

"Nigga, I'll break yo face!" Animal Cuz said, as he walked towards D-Red.

D-Red pulled out a .38 revolver, stopping him dead in his tracks.

"Oh, you gone pull a strap on me, motherfucker? Nigga, you better use it," Animal Cuz said.

"Don't push me," D-Red replied.

"You got that," Animal Cuz said, before walking out of the apartment.

When he got downstairs, his man, Stretch, was talking to some jump-offs from around his way.

"Stretch, I need to holla at you."

Stretch walked over to his boy.

"What's up?" Stretch asked.

"This bitch-ass nigga D-Red just pulled a banger on me! You strapped?"

"Nah, you know I don't fuck with them guns."

"I'm gone kill this nigga," Animal Cuz replied before walking off.

*   *   *

It took Animal Cuz a couple of days to get his hands on a strap. A lot of niggas from his block knew he was fresh out and didn't want to see him go back to jail for beefing over a jump-off. But Animal Cuz didn't see it that way.

There was no way he was gone let some nigga get away with beating on his baby mother in front of his daughter, and pulling a banger on him. His cousin Buggy, gave him a .45 that had a body on it. Animal Cuz didn't care, because he planned to put a few more bodies on it, his self. Buggy earned his name because it wasn't a day that went by that he didn't have a banger on him with at least two fully loaded clips. Everybody knew he was bugged out so the name Buggy fit him.

*   *   *

D-Red walked up Belden Street with a black duffel bag full of heroin in his hand. As he got next to his whip, he felt a sharp blow to the back of his head. He dropped the bag and reached for his toast. Animal Cuz put the gun to the back of his head.

"Don't even think about it, motherfucker!" Animal Cuz said.

He took D-Red's gun, cash, jewels, and bag of drugs.

"You thought you was a real tough guy with that gun in ya hand, didn't ya?" Animal Cuz asked.

Tears ran down D-Red's face.

"You ready to die, nigga?"

Animal Cuz cocked back the gun. Monito ran out the building busting off a black 9mm at Animal Cuz. Animal Cuz shot back before taking off on foot. D-Red thought he was dead, when he heard the first shot go off. Monito ran over to D-Red.

"You okay, boss?" Monito asked.

"Yeah, I'm good," D-Red replied, nervously.

*   *   *

Animal Cuz had came up something serious off the lick. He was sitting on over $50,000 in cash and a

194

bagged up kilo of heroin. Dope was never his thing. But the way shit was moving, Animal Cuz was really thinking about changing his hustle.

He copped a crisp Lexus GS 300 and threw screens all through it. Word was spreading through the hood that Animal Cuz had laid D-Red down and was back on top. As he drove down Vine Street, he saw Daphny and two of her girls walking up the block. He pulled on the side of her and hung his jeweled up arm out of the car.

"Daphny, what's up?" Animal Cuz asked.

Daphny looked in the car and saw Animal Cuz. She smiled when she saw him.

"What's up, Justin?" Daphny asked.

"Come here."

Daphny walked over to the car. She was wearing some little ass shorts, a pair of white Uptowns, and a wife beater that showed off a lot of cleavage. Animal Cuz's dick got hard just thinking about how he used to fuck them big and juicy breasts.

"Where my baby girl at?" Animal Cuz asked.

"She's with my mother."

"Give her this for me."

Animal Cuz went in his pocket and pulled out a large stack of cash. He handed Daphny $300.

"You got something for me?" Daphny asked.

"Definitely."

"Where it's at?"

"You'll get it tonight."

Daphny blushed.

"Put my number in ya phone," Daphny said, as she grabbed it from his lap and programmed her number in it.

"I'm gone come scoop you up later. Make sure that clown-ass nigga ain't around."

"I don't fuck with him no more.

Animal Cuz turned up CNN *The War Report* album before pulling off.

Chapter 40

A black S-550 Benz sitting on dubs pulled up in West Brook Housing Projects with the music bumping *The Best of Max-B*. Candy walked out of her apartment shaking what her mama gave her. On her way towards the car, she was stopped by someone grabbing her arm.

"Candy, can I talk to you for a second?" Rondell asked.

"Rondell, we ain't got shit to talk about! Now, get your damn hands up off of me!" Candy demanded, with much attitude.

"Oh, it's like that, Candy? You gone just throw away what we had for that clown-ass nigga?"

"What part of it's over don't you understand, Rondell? I ain't fucking ya bum ass no more!"

"You don't mean that, Candy. Can I just get a chance to show you that I changed? Let me take you out to dinner."

"Negro, please! I wouldn't go out with your broke ass if you had the last dick on earth. Stay the hell away from my house, Rondell!"

"Bitch, fuck you!" Rondell barked, before spraying a half of a bottle of Ocean Spray cranberry juice all over her white Moschino outfit.

By this time, Jerome had made it out of the car and was in the process of finding out why this cat was holding up his Shorty, when he saw Rondell throw juice on Candy. Jerome ran up on Rondell and punched him in the face. He jacked him up against the wall with brute force.

"Yo, what the fuck is wrong with you, Fam? Disrespecting my girl like that? Nigga, I will kill your bitch ass out here!" Jerome yelled, as he continued to punch Rondell in his face viciously.

Rondell tried to loosen the grip Jerome had on him, but his efforts were useless. Jerome was on him like a lion on a gazelle. Rondell's face was full of blood. The hustlers on the block looked on in amusement, as Jerome beat the brakes off of Rondell. They never really liked Rondell anyway, because he was always beating on Candy.

"Nigga, the next time you see Candy, you better go in the opposite direction and keep it moving! Don't let me see your bitch ass around here again! I won't be so lenient next time!" Jerome said, as he flashed his Desert Eagle in Rondell's face, letting him know he had just spared his life.

But like the Mob says, never show ya heat and don't flame it. Jerome got about 3 feet away before Rondell pulled out an all-black .45 automatic and started clapping.

Boom! Boom! Boom! Boom!

The first two shots missed Jerome, making him spin around and point his gat in Rondell's direction. He didn't get a shot off before he was hit in the leg once. Jerome let off two wild shots that didn't hit anything but sent Rondell running up the block, still busting off shots at Jerome, who was now laying on the ground, bleeding profusely.

"Oh my God! Baby, you need to go to the hospital," Candy said, nervously.

"Here, put this in the house," Jerome said, as he passed her his gun and a stack of cash.

Candy hid the gun and drugs in her apartment and called an ambulance. When they finally arrived, Jerome was put on a stretcher and brought to the hospital.

*   *   *

Unique and Melony rushed to their girl's aid, when they heard about Jerome getting shot.

"We got here as soon as we heard the news," Unique said, as she hugged Candy.

"Why is this happening to me? Just when I find a good man, something fucked up like this had to happen," Candy cried.

"Who shot him?"

"Rondell."

Unique sucked her teeth.

"This shit is getting out-of-control. Do you want me to have D-Red get rid of Rondell for you?" Unique asked.

Candy waited a few minutes in heavy thought before responding.

"Yes," Candy replied, as she wiped the tears from her face.

"I got you, girl," Unique replied.

*   *   *

D-Red stood on Belden Street, when he got a call from Unique.

"Hello?" D-Red said.

"Baby, where you at?"

199

"On the block, why, what's up?"

"I need to talk to you. I'm on my way."

"All right, come to the building."

Unique pulled up on Belden Street in her Benz. She jumped out of the car and walked to the building. All eyes were on her, as she walked across the street. She was looking right in some Grown & Sexy jeans with the t-shirt to match. Unique hugged D-Red when she stepped into the building.

"What's up?" D-Red asked.

"You know my friend, Candy?"

"Yeah, what about her?"

"Her ex-boyfriend, Rondell, has been stalking her and shot her boyfriend, Jerome, yesterday, because she wouldn't take him back," Unique informed him.

"What that gotta do with me?" D-Red asked, getting irritated with the conversation.

"I told her that you would take care of it."

"What?" D-Red asked, getting angrier by the second.

"Please, baby, do it for me. You know Candy is my best friend. And if something happened to her, I wouldn't be able to live with myself knowing that I could have helped prevent it."

"I'll see what I can do," D-Red said, reluctantly.

"Thank you, baby," Unique said, before kissing him on the lips.

D-Red watched, as she left the building. He was mad as hell that Unique had involved him in a murder. His cell phone rung, taking him out of his thoughts.

"Hello," D-Red said.

"We outside, playboy," Ghetto said.

"All right."

D-Red walked outside with the duffel bag full of cash. He jumped in the backseat of Ghetto's Cadillac truck. D-Red passed Ghetto the bag full of cash.

"I got something that I need y'all to take care of," D-Red said.

"What's up?" Ghetto asked.

"A kid named Rondell from Bowles Park been harassing a friend of mine's. I need him clipped."

"That's gone be $10,000."

"It's all in the bag," D-Red mumbled.

"I heard about that nigga, Animal Cuz, laying you down. You want us to take care of that, too?"

"Nah, that shit is personal," D-Red replied, before jumping out of the whip.

"All right, playboy, I got you."

Chapter 41

Rondell was labeled the black sheep of his family. He had burned all his bridges at an early age. The only person who was willing to take him in was his aunt, Jackie. His aunt had a daughter named Peggy that was the same age as Rondell.

She would walk around the house in her panties and t-shirts, doing things to turn him on. It didn't take Rondell long to try his hand with Peggy. It was a Sunday, and his aunt, Jackie, had just left for church. Rondell walked into Peggy's room. She had just got out of the shower and was applying lotion to her naked body.

"What you doing in here?" Peggy asked.

"I came to see you," Rondell replied, with a smile on his face.

"You know, if my mother catches you in here, it's gone be trouble."

"She just left for church," Rondell replied, as he walked over to his cousin and began kissing her.

She kissed him back. Rondell unbuckled his pants and let them fall to the floor, before penetrating her love box. She was real loose, as Rondell slid up in her box. Peggy began to moan, as Rondell beat the pussy up.

"Oh, fuck me!" Peggy moaned.

Rondell stroked faster and faster, making the bed squeak with every stroke. Rondell's aunt, Jackie, walked back into the house. She had forgotten her fan and had to have it, because the church didn't have any air conditioners.

As she walked upstairs, she heard a squeaking noise coming from Peggy's room. She opened up the door and walked in. Rondell's aunt, Jackie, couldn't believe her eyes, when she saw Peggy and Rondell both naked, fucking like jack rabbits.

"Rondell!" Jackie yelled, as he continued to fuck his cousin.

Peggy tried to pull away when she heard her mother. But it was no stopping Rondell until he got his nut off. Jackie couldn't believe the disrespect Rondell was showing her. By the time Rondell had fixed his clothes and walked out the room, his aunt had half of his clothes out the window.

"I will not tolerate disrespect and incest in this family, or in my own home! Get the rest of your shit and get the hell out of my home!" Jackie yelled.

Rondell grabbed the rest of his belongings and called up Candy. He let her know he needed a place to stay, because his aunt had kicked him out. He left out the small detail about him sleeping with his own cousin. Candy was there for her man in his time of need, and welcomed him into her home.

For the first few weeks of them living together, everything was going great, until he got comfortable. Rondell began staying out all night, sleeping with different women, stealing Candy's money, blowing it on weed and liquor, and flirting with damn near half the women in the project.

Word got back to Candy that Rondell had slept with Nancy, the project jump-off. Candy confronted Nancy about it, and she didn't deny anything. A big fist fight broke out right in the project, and Candy ended up mopping the floor with Nancy.

As for Rondell, he was right back on the streets. But this time, Candy was done with him. She told him it was over. But Rondell wasn't taking no for an answer. He was sprung for real. With no place to go, and his pockets on empty, Rondell turned to his best friend, Darnell, who was a part-time weed dealer and part-time student at Capital Community College.

"Rondell, what's up, man? You ain't looking too good," Darnell said.

"Man, my girl just kicked me out. I ain't got no place to go. I'm doing bad right now," Rondell said.

"Why she kick you out?"

"Somehow she found out I was messing around on her with this jump-off named Nancy from her project."

"Come on, Rondell. You know better than to shit where you lay. You know how females talk," Darnell lectured him.

"Yeah, I fucked up big-time. Ya boy needs a place to crash for a couple of days. Just until I figure out my next move."

"Come on, Rondell. You know I ain't tripping about you staying here. I got an extra room in the back."

"Good looking out, Darnell. When I get back on my feet, I'm gone pay you back."

Darnell looked at his watch.

"Yo, I gotta go to school. Make yourself at home."

It had been over six months since Darnell and Rondell had that conversation, and Rondell was still there. He hadn't found a job, or paid any rent, since he got there. Rondell was taken out of his thoughts when he heard a beeping horn in front of his building.

He looked outside and saw an E-Class Benz sitting on chrome dubs, parked in front of the building. Rondell recognized the driver of the Benz. It's Cee, an up-and-coming crack dealer from Albany Avenue who was making a name for his self in the game.

He had just moved into the building about two weeks ago with his beautiful wife, Precious. What Rondell would do to sample her goodies. At 5'4", Precious had a body like the porn star, Pinky, a cute face, dimples, brown eyes, and a walk that's mean.

Rondell began to get aroused, as he watched Precious from his window. And before he knew it, he was stroking his dick as he lusted over her. Precious bent down to grab a magazine that she just dropped, and Rondell sped up his pace, stroking his dick until he released his babies all over his fist and the floor, as he thought about Candy. He grabbed a towel and cleaned up the mess, as he continued to fill his brain with naughty thoughts of Precious.

Chapter 42

Silk and Ghetto cruised down Blue Hills Avenue with murder on their minds, and big guns on their laps.

"Where we supposed to find this clown-ass nigga, Rondell?" Ghetto asked, as he scanned the hood.

"Knowing that nigga, he might be up in one of them strip clubs with his freaky ass. I was locked up with the nigga one time in the Meadows. And all that nigga used to do is beat off to every female staff member up in the joint.

"This nigga didn't care if a chick was fat, old, ugly, or cute. He was gunning them bitches down like they were one of them Straight Stunting chicks. That nigga's vicious. They locked his dumb ass up in Seg for that shit, and I heard he was still beating off to them bitches when they came through to do their rounds."

"Freak nigga there."

Silk and Ghetto both started laughing.

"Yo, pull over!" Ghetto yelled.

Silk hit the brakes and Ghetto was out of the car with his gun in-hand, as fast as lightning. Before Silk could get out of the car, Ghetto was all over his victim, pistol-whipping him viciously.

"Nigga, didn't I tell you not to be out here unless you got my money?" Ghetto asked, as he continued to pistol-whip the man.

The man tried to cover up his big-ass head, but Ghetto wasn't having it. He brutally pistol-whipped the man with a .50 cal.

"Ghetto, I swear. I been trying to pay you. But I haven't been seeing you."

"Nigga, you got the motherfucking number! What? You take me for a fool? You trying to play me?"

"Ghetto, I ain't trying to play you. Check in my pocket. It's all there!" the man said, as he tried to block the blow from the gun that made another gash on the side of his head.

"I should murk yo bitch ass right here for thinking you can play with my money!"

"Please don't shoot me, Ghetto! We boys, man!"

"Nigga, you a motherfucking joke. You ain't my blood type. Get your punk ass out of here before I change my mind!"

Ghetto kicked the man in the ass for good measure, making him stumble a bit as he ran off.

"Next week, you better have my motherfucking money, or it's lights out, nigga!" Ghetto yelled at the fleeing man.

Silk laughed, as he jumped back in the car.

"Why you do that nigga like that?" Silk asked, while laughing.

"I told that bitch-ass nigga not to play with my bread. But he wanna keep testing my gangster, ducking me and shit whenever I come through. He lucky I ain't murk his bitch ass!" Ghetto said, as he punched his right hand into the palm of his left hand.

"Sometimes all these niggas respect is violence.

*   *   *

Lil Crimey and Real Deal walked down the War Zone. They stopped dead in their tracks when they saw Police Statements stapled up against the light pole.

"What the fuck is this, Blood?" Lil Crimey asked, as he snatched the Police Statement from the pole.

As he began reading the Police Statement, he realized that Nashelle was telling on Block, a young shooter from the Ave who had a rep on the streets for putting that work in. Lil Crimey frowned his face up when he was done reading the Police Statement.

"This bitch, Nashelle, is telling, Blood," Lil Crimey said.

"Let me see that," Real Deal said.

Real Deal read the Police Statement, also, and shook his head when he was done.

"Nashelle ain't right."

"She going against everything I believe in right now."

"So what we gone do?"

"I got this," Lil Crimey replied, before walking off.

*   *   *

Nashelle sat in her apartment on Money Martin watching *The Maury Show*. The guests were arguing about whether or not he was the father.

"That's his baby!" Nashelle said out loud to herself.

She was laying on her couch in a pair of shorts and a t-shirt. Her front door was open, but the screen door was closed to let some air in the house. She didn't have air conditioner. So it was always hot up in her crib. Lil Crimey walked into her apartment. Nashelle jumped when he stepped into the living room.

"Ooh, boy, you scared me. Creeping up on me like that," Nashelle said.

208

Lil Crimey had a serious look on his face.

"Boy, what's wrong with you?" Nashelle asked.

"Why you do it?" Lil Crimey asked.

"Do what?

Lil Crimey smacked Nashelle in the face with the Police Statement. Nashelle read the Statement before replying.

"I thought you would be happy I put that nigga behind bars. You don't fuck with him anyway, right?

"Bitch, what's done in the streets stays in the streets!" Lil Crimey said, before shooting Nashelle in the forehead with a .357 revolver.

The roar of the gun was loud and intimidating. He threw on his black hood and crept out the backdoor of her apartment.

Chapter 43

Kayo drove up Blue Hills with the music bumping. He had *The Best of Cormega* bumping, when he pulled up on a young hustler named G-Rock. G-Rock jumped in the car, agitated.

"What took you so long?" G-Rock asked, before passing Kayo $1,350.

Kayo passed G-Rock 2 ounces and a quarter of crack. The boy jumped out of the car and walked into his building. Kayo got a phone call.

"Hello?" Kayo said.

"Meet me on Palm Street. You know what time it is! It's black taxes," Silk said to Kayo, before hanging up.

*   *   *

Melony stood at her station in the beauty salon washing her client's hair, when Shantae walked in looking like she had seen better days. She was a hot mess. As she walked past Melony, she ice grilled her. Melony ice grilled her right back before speaking her mind.

"You got an eye problem?" Melony asked.

"Yeah, bitch! I should beat yo ass for fucking with my man!" Shantae said, as she ran up on Melony and caught her with a right hook to the side of her face.

Melony snatched Shantae by her hair and began to punch her in the face. Ms. Buchanan stepped out of her office looking sexy as hell in a bodysuit made by Grown

& Sexy. She was in her 40s and resembled the beautiful actress, Wendy Raquel Robinson.

"Y'all break that up! Y'all ain't gone be tearing up my shit," Ms. Buchanan said.

The hair stylist broke up the fight.

"This shit ain't over! When I see you in the streets, it's on!" Shantae threatened.

"Bitch, you know where I be," Melony replied.

"Get her out of here! Melony, in my office now!" Ms. Buchanan said.

The hair stylist escorted Shantae out of the hair salon and locked the door.

"Bitch, you gotta come out of there sometime! And when you do, I'm gone beat that ass again!" Shantae said, from outside.

Melony walked to the back office where Ms. Buchanan was at.

"Yes, Ms. Buchanan."

"Melony, what's up with you? Sleeping with another woman's man?"

"Ms. Buchanan, with all due respect, what I do in my private life is nobody's business."

"It is, when you bring it into my shop."

"I was not aware that Ray was still with her."

"Ray? No, you mean Eddie. Ray left her ass a few months ago," Ms. Buchanan corrected her.

"The only man I have been with in over a year is Mr. Ray Black."

"That child is around here fighting over a man that is not even with her anymore. She was in front of the shop about three months ago yelling and carrying on when he told her he was done with her," Ms. Buchanan said.

"I'm sorry that I brought drama into your shop."

"It's not your fault. Shantae is just jealous and ignorant. Out here fighting over some dick that don't even belong to her no more."

Melony and Ms. Buchanan shared a laugh before Melony went back to her station. Besides a small scratch on her face, Melony was good.

*   *   *

Mr. Ray Black picked Melony up from Flava's Beauty Salon in his Murcielago. She had a bad attitude and Mr. Ray Black was concerned.

"What's the matter with you, Melony?"

"Ya bitch came to the shop today. I had to beat her ass!" Melony said.

"Who are you talking about?"

"Shantae."

Mr. Ray Black sighed.

"It has been over between me and Shantae for months."

"I know. Ms. Buchanan told me."

"I'm going to check her ass for that. Are you okay?" Mr. Ray Black asked.

"I'm good. But her face ain't," Melony replied.

Mr. Ray Black dialed Shantae's number. She answered on the second ring.

"Hey, baby," Shantae said.

"Don't hey baby me! I heard about what you did today, and I don't appreciate you stepping to my woman!"

"Your woman? What about us?"

"There is no us, Shantae. Those days are over!" Mr. Ray Black corrected her.

Shantae cried into the phone.

"Fuck you, Ray! You black motherfucker!" Shantae yelled into the phone, before Mr. Ray Black hung up on her.

Melony smiled in the passenger's seat. She had got the last laugh and the man to go with it.

Chapter 44

Rondell walked into the hallway when he saw Precious walk into the building. She was at her mailbox when he walked up and checked his mail, also.

"Good afternoon," Rondell said.

"Good afternoon," Precious replied.

"I couldn't help but notice that book you're reading. Are you a writer?" Rondell asked.

"Yes."

"What type of books do you write?"

"Urban fiction," Precious stated.

"Word?"

"Yeah.

"Well, if you ever run out of material, I have a hell of a story for you," Rondell suggested.

"I'll keep that in mind."

Rondell handed her his phone number before walking back upstairs.

*   *   *

Melony, Candy, and Unique drove down Martin Street in Unique's Benz. A young boy no older than 15 flagged them down. He had some flyers in his hand.

"What's up, little man?" Unique asked.

"This flyer is for my boy, Richard Warren's, book release party," the boy replied, before passing the girls flyers.

"Good looking out."

"No doubt," the boy replied, before running up on the next car that was behind them.

Unique looked at the flyer and saw the cover for Richard Warren's latest book titled *The Diamond Family*.

"Y'all going to the book release party?" Unique asked.

"Nah, I gotta make sure Jerome is okay," Candy replied.

"Girl, he will be all right for a few hours. He's already back on his feet and everything," Unique said.

"Let me call him and see if he's good."

Candy dialed Jerome's number on her cell phone.

"Hello?" Jerome said.

"Bay, where you at?" Candy asked.

"At the gym, exercising my leg. Why? What's up?"

"I wanted to know if it was all right for me to go to Richard Warren's book release party tonight?"

"Yeah, why not? I'm going," Jerome answered.

"Thank you, baby. I love you."

"I love you, too."

"Bye."

Candy hung up the phone.

"We gotta go shopping," Candy said.

Unique and Melony both smiled and were happy that their girl wasn't down like she had been for the last couple of weeks due to Jerome getting shot. They went to the Buckland Hills Mall to get fly. Their first stop was the Gucci store, where they got a few designer dresses, shoes, handbags, and shades.

After blowing a couple of dollars at the mall, the ladies went home, showered, and got dressed. They were killing them when they stepped in the book release party,

Gucci down to their shoes. The party was full of entertainers, athletes, ballers, hustlers, and fly honeys.

Everybody had come out to show love to Hartford's finest, Richard Warren. He was dressed in an all-white Prada suit with the hard-bottom Prada shoes to match. His waves were on spin, and he was the life of the party.

He took pictures with all of his fans and signed autographs. He even performed a few tracks off of his latest album, *Homicide Hartford*. Everyone who had came out had a good time and couldn't wait for the next one.

Chapter 45

Jerome and Candy walked through Elizabeth Park holding hands on a nice summer day. They were enjoying the weather and each other's company, when Clareese, a friend of Lisa's, saw them together.

"Jerome, what's up? How's my girl, Lisa?" Clareese asked.

"She's doing okay," Jerome replied.

"Can I speak with you in private for a second, Jerome?" Clareese asked.

"Give me one second," Jerome told Candy, before walking over to Clareese.

"What's up?" Jerome asked.

"You serious, Jerome? My girl gets locked up and you go out and start cheating on her? This ya new girlfriend?" Clareese asked.

"It ain't even like that," Jerome replied.

"Well, it damn sure seems like that," Clareese said, before walking away with a you know I'm telling look on her face.

'Damn', Jerome said in his mind, as he walked back over to Candy.

*   *   *

Lisa sat in the dayroom playing a game of chess with Sister Morgan, when the Correctional Officer called her name for mail.

"Right here," Lisa said, as she got up and grabbed her letter.

She looked at the name of the letter and sucked her teeth. It was the first time she had gotten mail from her so-called friend, Clareese. Lisa opened the letter and began reading it. The letter said:

Dear Lisa,

I'm sorry that I haven't been writing you like a true friend is supposed to, but I just don't seem to have the time to sit down and write you a letter about all of the bullshit that is going on in the world.

But today is different. I saw Jerome in Elizabeth Park the other day all hugged up with some chick named Candy. You might remember her. Tammy said she used to go to school with us. But I don't remember her. I just thought you should know that, Lisa.

Love, Clareese

A single tear dropped down on the letter, as Lisa read the last line. What she had been thinking all this time had been confirmed. She walked to her cell before anyone could see her break down and cry.

"Lisa, what's wrong?" Joselyn asked.

"Jerome is cheating on me," Lisa replied, as she wiped her eyes.

Joselyn put the *XXL* magazine she was reading down and hopped off of her bed. She was wearing a pair of shorts that hugged her thighs and ass just right. Her fat camel toe could also be seen, while she wore the shorts.

"Come here, girl," Joselyn said.

She sat down on the bed next to Lisa and held her.

"It's gone be all right," Joselyn assured her.

Lisa looked into Joselyn's eyes. She looked so beautiful, and Lisa was in need of someone to love her. She kissed Joselyn. Joselyn kissed her back, as she felt on Lisa's large breasts. Correctional Officer Green looked into the window and saw the women engaging in sexual activities.

He immediately became aroused, as they had oral sex in the 69 position. Keisha Cole bumped through the Koss large headphones, as they brought each other to ecstasy.

Chapter 46

Precious laid in her bed in a pair of sweatpants and a t-shirt. She had her laptop on her lap, but was having a bad case of writer's block. She looked at the card Rondell had given her. It said "Rondell's Auto Body". She debated on whether or not she should call him.

Eventually, she ended up giving him a call. Rondell turned down the volume on *Big Booty Hoes* Vol. 3, when he heard the phone ringing.

"Hello?" Jerome said.

"Hey, this is Precious.

"Hey, what's up, Precious? How you doing?"

"Not too good," Precious whined.

"What seems to be the problem?"

"I'm having a bad case of writer's block."

"Well, like I told you before, I got a hell of a story for you. Do you need me to come over?" Jerome asked, anxiously.

"I don't think my boyfriend would like another man in his home. But you can tell it to me over the phone."

"That's cool. Well, it all started out like this."

Rondell began to break down his life story. He was talking in third person, because he knew if he confessed his true self to her, she would never speak to him again. By the end of the night, Precious had about five chapters done.

She was truly grateful to Rondell, because her publisher had been pressuring her to drop another book. Her first book was titled *Double Life*. It was an urban erotica about a stripper who lived a double life. She was a stripped at night, and a secretary for a very important businessman during the day. The book sold off the shelves, and her fans were looking for that next hit.

"Rondell, thank you so much for helping me out with my book," Precious said.

"No problem. Call me tomorrow, so we can start where we left off."

"All right."

Precious hung up the phone and fell asleep. Rondell cleaned his self off. He had been beating off, while he talked to Precious on the phone all night. And she hadn't even realized it.

*   *   *

Rondell walked down Albany Avenue, headed to the store, when he felt like someone was behind him. He looked back and saw Ghetto with a black hood, covering his head, walking towards him real fast. Rondell took off running.

Ghetto pulled out a black 9mm and started busting at Rondell. Rondell swerved the bullets and ran straight up Magnolia and into the Police Station.

"Damn!" Ghetto said, as he tucked his hammer and got up out of there.

Rondell was breathing heavy, as he stood at the front desk.

"Are you okay, son?" Detective Jennings asked.

"No! Somebody just tried to kill me!"

"Come with me, son."

The Police circled the area looking for Suspects that matched the description that Rondell had given them, but didn't find anyone. Rondell looked through the mug shots.

"That's him! That's the guy who tried to kill me!" Rondell said.

Detective Jennings looked at the photo.

"His name is Terrel Reed aka Ghetto but uses lots of alias when he's locked up. He runs with this man, Jeffrey Washington aka Silk. We've been looking for these two men for quite some time now. They were hit men for the Commission and murdered a lot of people."

"Why would they want to kill me?" Rondell asked.

"That's a question you have to ask yourself," Detective Jennings replied.

Rondell thought long and hard, but couldn't come up with an answer. Detective Jennings drove him home.

"If you see Silk or Ghetto again, don't hesitate to give me a call."

"All right, thanks, Detective."

"No problem."

*　　*　　*

Ghetto was mad as hell that he had blown his shot at murdering Rondell.

"This bitch-ass nigga ran up in the motherfucking Police Station!" Ghetto said.

"That nigga went in there and spilled the beans," Silk replied.

"When I catch up with that nigga, I'm gone punish his rat ass!" Ghetto replied.

*　　*　　*

Precious talked on the phone with Rondell, getting the final pages of her book done. They had been kicking it on the phone for the last two weeks.

"Rondell, you just don't know how much of a lifesaver you are," Precious said.

"How about we have one drink to celebrate the completion of your new book."

"I don't know."

"Come on, Precious. One drink won't hurt."

"Let me get dressed," Precious said.

She put on a pair of 7 jeans, a white blouse, and a pair of Nine West boots, before walking down the hall to Rondell's apartment. Rondell let her in and offered her a seat on the couch. He had the lights dim and Avant's CD playing on the CD player. He poured them both a glass of Asti Spumante.

"So how does it feel to finally be done with your book?" Rondell asked.

"It feels good. I wouldn't have been able to do it without you."

"Let's make a toast to much success on your new book."

They tapped champagne glasses and drank the champagne. One glass turned into a couple more. And before Precious knew it, they were kissing. Precious pulled back after a few moments.

"I can't do this. I'm sorry," Precious said, as she left his apartment.

"Precious, hold on a second," Rondell called to her.

But she was gone, leaving Rondell with a hard dick and no chick. He was tired of beating off and needed a woman in his life. He hadn't been out of the house in two weeks, since Silk and Ghetto tried to murk him.

He looked out his window and saw a bad-ass red-bone chick standing across the street, prostituting. She had on an extra tight miniskirt, a halter top that showed off her large breasts, and some fire red fuck-me pumps on her feet. Rondell couldn't believe his luck. He rushed out the crib and called the girl over.

"Hey, what's up, baby? You working?" Rondell asked.

"That all depends on what you spending," the girl replied, with much sass in her voice.

"How about $20?"

"How about yo broke ass get a crack whore?" the girl replied before she started walking away.

"Hold up, ma. Don't be so fast to turn down money. How about $30?"

"Forty dollars."

"All right, I can do that. Let's go in the building," Rondell stated.

"I need to see the money first."

As Rondell dug in his pocket for his last $40 Ghetto crept up on him with a large Champion hood over his head.

"Lights out, playboy!" Ghetto said, before he pulled the trigger and blew half of Rondell's brains all over the girl.

The girl started to scream as the body dropped. Ghetto silenced her with two bullets to the face. He jumped back in the rental and Silk pulled off. Ghetto knew Rondell sex addiction would eventually be the same thing that would kill him in the end.

224

Ghetto had paid the pretty young prostitute/stripper to stand in front of the building, until Rondell asked her for sex. The stripper didn't know murder would be involved. So when she saw Rondell get his brains blown out, she went hysterical.

Chapter 47

Lil Crimey walked into his family reunion down in South Carolina. He saw his cousins, aunts, and uncles that he hadn't seen in years. He had a drink in his hand as his uncle showed him around to all his cousins, aunts, and uncles.

When Lil Crimey and his uncle walked over to where Silk was sitting, World War II almost popped off at the family reunion. Lil Crimey reached for his hammer, but realized it wasn't there. Silk did the same.

"Nigga, I'll beat yo ass!" Lil Crimey said.

"You ain't ready!" Silk replied as he set up on Lil Crimey.

"Hold up now! Ain't gone be no fighting up in here! Not amongst family," Uncle David said.

"That nigga ain't my blood type," Lil Crimey said angrily.

"Word!" Silk agreed.

"You fools is first cousins. Silk is Randy's son and Lil Crimey is your uncle, Joshua's, son."

"That nigga ain't no kin to Uncle Randy," Lil Crimey said.

"Look at him! That boy is the splitting image of his daddy."

"If he is family, how come I ain't never seen him before now?"

"Because his mama stop dealing with Uncle Randy."

Lil Crimey looked at Silk and had to admit he did look just like his pops. Uncle Randy was Lil Crimey's favorite uncle. He had taught him how to fight, ride a bike, and how to tie his shoelaces when his real father wasn't around.

He knew his uncle would be turning in his grave if he knew him and Silk were out on the streets beefing. Uncle Randy had died in a prison riot back in 1995. To say Lil Crimey was hurting would be an understatement.

"Whatever beef y'all two had on the streets ends here!" Uncle David said.

The two men stared each other down before Lil Crimey gave Silk a hug.

"Welcome to the family, Blood!" Lil Crimey said.

"It's all love," Silk replied.

They hung out for the rest of the day getting high and drunk before they parted ways.

*　　*　　*

Lisa laid on her bunk thinking of ways to make Candy and Jerome pay for crossing her. She couldn't believe that Candy would stoop so low as to sleep with her man. Lisa made a promise that she would make them both feel it when she got out.

*　　*　　*

D-Red sat parked in front of Daphny's apartment. He had been blowing her phone up all night. But she wasn't answering none of his calls. She had been acting real shady since her baby father had come home and D-Red wasn't feeling that shit at all.

He tried her number again, and it went straight to voicemail. As he was about to get out the car and go

upstairs he saw Animal Cuz and Daphny drive down 252.
Animal Cuz and D-Red locked eyes. Animal Cuz smiled
and kept driving.

D-Red was heated when he saw Daphny with
Animal Cuz. He went into a jealous rage and peeled off
behind them. Animal Cuz sped up, but D-Red was on
him in the Benz. When they got next to the corner store
D-Red crashed into Animal Cuz at full speed.

Both cars flipped over. Animal Cuz climbed out
the window as he shook off the impact of the car crash.
As he ran to the other side to grab his baby mother the
car exploded. Animal Cuz flew back from the impact of
the explosion.

"No!" Animal Cuz yelled, as he watched his baby
mother, Daphny, get blown to pieces.

Tears fell down his eyes as he pulled out his .38
revolver and walked over to D-Red's car. D-Red was
struggling, trying to get out the car when Animal Cuz
popped three shots into his face.

"Die, motherfucker! Die!" Animal Cuz yelled
before tucking the gun in his waistband and fleeing the
scene.

*   *   *

Unique was at her home with her mother when
Candy came to the house.

"Hey, what's up, girl?" Unique asked.

"They killed D-Red and Daphny," Candy said,
before she broke down and started crying.

"What?" Unique asked, not fully comprehending
what was just said to her.

228

"It's been on the news for the last past half-hour," Candy replied.

Unique flicked to the news and saw the gruesome scene.

"Oh my, God! Mama, why me?" Unique yelled, before she broke down in her mother's arms.

"We gone get through this, baby," Valerie said, as she held her daughter in her arms.

*   *   *

D-Red and Daphny's funeral was packed with family, loved ones, and friends. Everyone had come out to pay their respects to the dead. Unique had fell into a deep state of depression and began to isolate herself. She didn't want to be bothered with anyone, and rarely talked anymore.

She was definitely hurting. Not only did she lose her man, but she had lost her cousin, as well, and the killer was still on the loose.

Chapter 48

<u>One Year Later</u>

Unique pulled up at Bernice's in her brand-new Aston Martin. She was looking sexy as hell in a Grown & Sexy skirt set that showed off her thick and chocolate thighs. She was looking good, as hell, and niggas was on her. Unique ignored their sexual advances, as she stepped into the restaurant.

"Welcome to Bernice's. How may I help you?" Carl asked.

"Let me get a steak and rice, and peas meal, with extra dumplings, and a carrot juice," Unique said.

Carl took her order. A few minutes later, her meal was done.

"Your order is ready. That will be $10," Carl said.

Unique looked in her purse for her cash, but couldn't find her money.

"I left my cash in my other bag," Unique said.

"I got this," Animal Cuz said, as he placed a $10 bill on the counter.

Unique looked up and smiled, when she saw how handsome and well-built he was.

"Thank you," she said.

"You don't remember me?"

"No," Unique replied.

"Me and Daphny have a daughter together."

"You must be Animal Cuz?"

"Yeah, that's me," Animal Cuz stated.

"How do you deal with losing Daphny?"

"I take it one day at a time, Unique," Animal Cuz replied, before he began to walk out of the restaurant.

"Hey, wait."

Animal Cuz turned around.

"I'm not doing nothing, and I just got the complete season of *Hood Politics*," Unique replied.

Animal Cuz smiled.

*   *   *

"Oh, fuck me!" Unique moaned, as Animal Cuz dug all up in her guts.

It had been over a year since the last time she had sex, and she was in desperate need of some good dick. Animal Cuz explored places that she thought she only knew about. He was long-dicking her and making her cum all over his pipe. Animal Cuz stroked faster and faster, as she started gushing. He came right after her.

"Ah, yes, baby, I'm cumming," he said, as he skeeted off.

Unique and Animal Cuz laid in each other's arms, enjoying one another's presence, as they got lifted on purple haze and watched *Hood Politics*.

*   *   *

Unique and Animal Cuz had been dating strong for about three months, and Unique was really feeling him. Animal Cuz treated her special and knew all the right words to say to make her want him. Unique decided to treat her man to a few outfits at the mall.

She had just put it on him, and left him knocked out at the apartment. As she walked into Filene's, she saw Calvin. But he didn't bother to speak to her.

"What's up, Calvin?" Unique asked.

Calvin looked her up and down with disgust all over his face before walking into Filene's.

Unique followed him into the store.

"Calvin, did I miss something here? What was all that about?"

Don't act like you don't know what that's about! You running around town fucking the nigga who killed D-Red!" Calvin said.

"What? I swear I didn't know!" Unique said, as tears filled up in her eyes.

Calvin looked into her eyes and could tell that her words were sincere. Calvin hugged her.

"You gotta stop fucking with that nigga. He's no good," Calvin said.

"I will."

*   *   *

Animal Cuz laid in his bed at his apartment watching music videos, when he heard the key turn in the door.

"That's you, baby?" Animal Cuz asked, with a smile on his face.

He got no response, but heard the Grown & Sexy high heels Unique was wearing click with every step she took. Unique's walk was mean. When she stepped into the bedroom, she held an all-black .380 automatic in her hand.

She shot Animal Cuz in the chest three times. The smile on his face quickly turned into a look of shock, as he gasped for air. Unique walked out of his apartment just as sexy as she stepped into it.

Chapter 49

Jerome kissed Candy on the lips.

"Baby, I'll be back in a little while. I gotta go handle some business," Jerome said.

"Okay, baby. I love you and be careful," Candy replied.

"I will."

Jerome left the house in his black Lexus SC 300. In the trunk of his car, he had over 6 kilos of cocaine. His young boy, Money Grip, had just ran out of product and needed to drop off a few packages to his workers. Jerome never got his hands dirty doing the hand-to-hand thing.

He dealt with one cat, and let him flood the streets with product. Jerome had learned that from his cousin, Majic, who had shit on smash down in Atlanta. A large majority of the work was coming through him. But nobody knew it besides him and his cousin.

Jerome turned up *jadakiss* on the CD deck, before hitting the highway. Candy stepped into her living room, when she felt someone grab her. She fought with her attacker. They both fell on top of a glass table, making it shatter.

Candy clawed at her attacker's face, who was wearing a ski mask, an all-black hoodie, and pants. She was able to snatch the mask off of her attacker's face.

"Lisa?" Candy said.

"Yeah, bitch! It's me! You thought I was gone let you get away with fucking my man? Not in this lifetime!"

"I never meant for it to go down like this," Candy admitted.

"Bitch, we was supposed to be home girls. And this is how you crossed me?"

"I'm sorry."

"It's too late for apologies! The only thing that can make things right is yo blood on my knife!" Lisa said, as she pulled out a switchblade and advanced towards Candy.

Candy took off running down the steps. Lisa swung the blade, just missing Candy's legs. As Candy ran up the steps, Lisa tripped her. Candy fell. Lisa dragged her down the steps.

"Bitch, I'm gone make you hurt like I hurt for all that time!" Lisa said, as she lifted the knife in the air, ready to plunge it into Candy's chest.

"Drop the knife!" Sheriff Peters ordered, as she pointed her gun at Lisa.

Lisa attempted to stab Candy, but two slugs from Sheriff Peters' gun hit her in the head and neck, killing her instantly.

"Are you okay, ma'am?" Sheriff Peters asked.

"I am now," Candy replied, as she caught her breath.

THE END

In a hood like Homicide Hartford everybody wants to be the boss. The Black Al Capone leader of a vicious street crew from the Ave called Flamboyant Gangsters has his hood on smash. One altercation in the club leads to an all out war with the Holly Wood Crew. The fight quickly leads to bullets and gun smoke. Which crew will be victorious in this all out war?

BOSS OF THE GHETTO   RICHARD WARREN

BOSS OF THE GHETTO

RICHARD WARREN

HOOD LIT PUBLISHING PRESENTS

$TICK UP KID$ 2

$TICK UP KID$ 2

IS OUR HOOD?

This story takes place on the mean streets of Hartford Connecticut in the Stowe Village housing projects better known as Crook Ville. It's one of the most notorious housing projects in America.

With Wise serving a life sentence and his crew dead the Crook Ville housing projects are up for grabs.

It's a new set of dope slangis on the come up with plans of taking over, but Asia fresh home from doing a five year bid has plans of her own. With a crew of go hard chicks running behind her they form the Grimy Chicks clique and the city will never be the same. With a us against the world mentality the Grimy Chicks clique hit the streets hard robbing the biggest gangsters of the city. In a city where the price of life is cheap and one slip up could cost you everything will the Grimy Chicks clique rise to the top or fall like the stick up kids before them?

RICHARD McCARTHY

The Second of a Five Book Series.

236

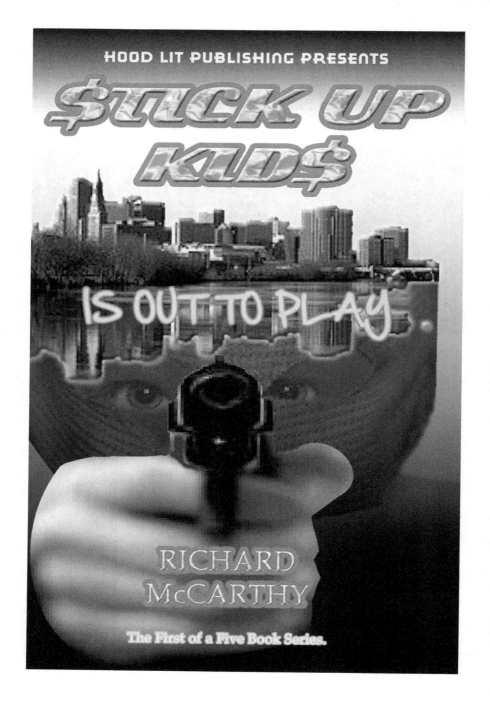

HOOD LIT PUBLISHING PRESENTS

$TICK UP KID$

IS OUT TO PLAY

RICHARD McCARTHY

The First of a Five Book Series.

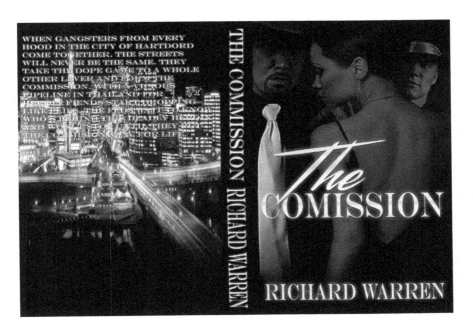

WHEN GANGSTERS FROM EVERY
HOOD IN THE CITY OF HARTDORD
COME TOGETHER. THE STREETS
WILL NEVER BE THE SAME. THEY
TAKE THE DOPE GAME TO A WHOLE
OTHER LEVER AND FORM THE
COMMISSION. WITH A VICIOUS
PIPELINE IN THAILAND FOR
THEIR FIENDS START DROPPING
LIKE FLIES. THE FEDS WANT TO KNOW
WHO'S BEHIND THE DEADLY HEROIN.
AND WON'T STOP UNTIL THEY GET
THE COMMISSION AWAY FOR LIFE.

THE COMMISSION RICHARD WARREN

The
COMISSION

RICHARD WARREN

MAGNIFICENT A CRIMINAL AND MASTERMIND FROM
THE MEAN STREETS OF HARTFORD CT FORMS A
CREW OF GO HARD GANGSTERS TO TAKE OVER THE
DRUG TRADE IN THE CITY. HE WILL STOP AT
NOTHING TO GET WHAT HE WANTS. REPPING TIME A
RIVAL BOSS HAS THE CITY ON LOCK. WHEN THE TWO
BOSSES CLASH THE MURDER RATE ESCALATES TO
AN ALL TIME HIGH. AFTER THE SMOKE CLEARS
WHO WILL REIGN KING OF THESE EVIL STREETS?

THESE EVIL STREETS RICHARD WARREN

THESE
EVIL Streets

RICHARD WARREN

238